MOTHER'S DAY MURDER

A LUCY STONE MYSTERY

MOTHER'S DAY MURDER

LESLIE MEIER

THORNDIKE
CHIVERS

This Large Print edition is published by Thorndike Press, Waterville, Maine, USA and by BBC Audiobooks Ltd, Bath, England.
Thorndike Press, a part of Gale, Cengage Learning.
Copyright © 2009 by Leslie Meier.
The moral right of the author has been asserted.

LIBRARY OF CONGRESS CATALOGING-IN-PUBLICATION DATA

Meier, Leslie.
  Mother's Day murder : a Lucy Stone mystery / by Leslie Meier.
    p. cm. — (Thorndike Press large print mystery)
    ISBN-13: 978-1-4104-1662-9 (hardcover : alk. paper)
    ISBN-10: 1-4104-1662-3 (hardcover : alk. paper)
    1. Stone, Lucy (Fictitious character)—Fiction. 2. High school students—Fiction. 3. Mothers and daughters—Fiction. 4. Murder—Investigation—Fiction. 5. Maine—Fiction. 6. Large type books. I. Title.
PS3563.E3455M67 2009
813'.54—dc22   2009009203

BRITISH LIBRARY CATALOGUING-IN-PUBLICATION DATA AVAILABLE

Published in 2009 in the U.S. by arrangement with Kensington Books, and imprint of Kensington Publishing Corp.
Published in 2009 in the U.K. by arrangement with the author.

U.K. Hardcover: 978 1 408 45650 7 (Chivers Large Print)
U.K. Softcover: 978 1 408 45651 4 (Camden Large Print)

Printed in the United States of America
1 2 3 4 5 6 7 13 12 11 10 09

MOTHER'S DAY MURDER

CHAPTER ONE

The photo on the front page of the Sunday paper was familiar. NO MOTHER'S DAY FOR CORINNE'S MOM read the headline above the plump, sad-eyed woman holding a photo of her pretty teenage daughter. Lucy Stone didn't have to read the story; as a reporter for the weekly *Pennysaver* newspaper, she knew all about it. Corinne Appleton, who had a summer job working as a counselor for the town recreation program in nearby Shiloh, had disappeared minutes after her mother dropped her off at the park. The story had been front-page news for weeks, then had gradually slipped to page three and, finally, to the second section as other stories demanded attention. But now, ten months later, Corinne was still missing.

"How come you're looking so glum?" demanded her husband, Bill, as he entered the room. "Aren't you enjoying Mother's Day?"

Lucy quickly flipped over the paper, hiding Joanne Appleton's reproachful face.

"My mother always said Mother's Day was invented by the greeting card companies to boost sales," she said, beginning the struggle to get into a pair of control-top panty hose.

"I always heard it was a creation of the necktie manufacturers," complained Bill, who often declared he never regretted giving up suits and ties and Wall Street for the T-shirts and jeans he wore as a restoration carpenter in the little Maine town of Tinker's Cove. "I finally found this in the coat closet downstairs," he said, holding up a rather rumpled tie, the only one he possessed.

"If you think a tie is torture, you ought to try panty hose," said Lucy, who usually wore jeans and running shoes, practical attire for her job. Today she was squeezing into heels and a suit for a Mother's Day brunch at the fancy Queen Victoria Inn. "I don't want to seem ungrateful, but I liked it better when the kids gave me homemade cards and plants for the garden."

"And I'd cook breakfast, and you'd get to eat it in bed."

"Eventually," laughed Lucy. "I'd be starving by the time it actually arrived."

"That's because they had to pick the pansies and make the place mat and decorate the napkin," said Bill. "It was quite a production. And then they'd fight over who got to carry the tray." He looked across the bed at his wife, who was standing in front of her dresser, putting on a pair of earrings. "Those were the days," he said, crossing the room and slipping his arms around her waist and nuzzling her neck.

His beard, now speckled with gray, tickled, and Lucy smiled. "Those days are over," she said. "Our little nest is almost empty."

It was true. Only Sara, a high school freshman, and Zoe, in fifth grade, remained at home. Toby, their oldest, lived with his wife, Molly, and their son, eight-week-old Patrick, on neighboring Prudence Path. Elizabeth, their oldest daughter, was a student at Chamberlain College in Boston.

"Can you believe we're grandparents?" continued Lucy, tickling Bill's ear.

"You're still pretty hot," said Bill, appreciatively eyeing her trim figure and cap of glossy dark hair.

"It's a battle," sighed Lucy, leaning forward to smooth on her age-defying makeup.

Bill grabbed her hips and pressed against her, but Lucy wiggled free. "We'll be late," she said, reaching for her lipstick. "Besides, now that I'm actually in these panty hose, there's no chance they're coming off."

Bill sighed and headed for the door.

"But I appreciate the gesture," she added.

Out in the hallway Bill was knocking on the girls' bedroom doors. "Bus leaves in five minutes," he said. She heard him go downstairs, followed by the clatter of the girls in their dressy shoes.

Lucy was the last to join the group in the kitchen. Bill was handsome in his all-purpose navy blazer, the girls adorable in flowery dresses that bared their arms and shoulders. They'd freeze but there was no point telling them; they'd been planning what to wear for weeks, ever since Toby came up with the idea of treating his wife and mother to the Mother's Day brunch. "It's Molly's first Mother's Day," he'd said. "We should do something special."

Unspoken, Lucy suspected, was his concern for Molly, who was making a slow recovery from a difficult pregnancy that ended abruptly on St. Patrick's Day, several weeks earlier than expected. Little Patrick hadn't appreciated his sudden entry into the world and was a cranky and fussy baby, demanding all his exhausted mother's attention. Lucy helped as much as she could with household chores and meals, but only

Molly could breast-feed the hungry little fellow, who demanded a meal every couple of hours, day and night. Toby did his best to help, too, but he was putting in long hours on the boat, getting ready for lobster season.

The new parents were already seated when they arrived at the inn's sunny dining room. Patrick was propped in a baby seat between them, sound asleep.

"What an angel," cooed Lucy, stroking his downy cheek. Even in his sleep, his lips made little nursing motions.

"More like a barracuda," complained Molly. She was still pudgy from her pregnancy, her face was splotchy, and she needed a haircut. Nevertheless, she'd made an effort, and although she was still wearing maternity pants, she'd topped them with a pretty pastel sweater. Seeing her, Lucy was reminded of the terrifying days after Toby's birth, when she was afraid of dropping him on his head or sticking him with a diaper pin or starving him or overfeeding him and thereby proving her incompetence as a mother.

"The first three months are the hardest," said Lucy. "But you're obviously doing something right. He looks great."

"He's much too skinny," said Molly. "Even though I nurse him constantly, I don't think he's getting enough."

Lucy sat beside Molly and took her hand. "He just looks skinny to you, believe me," she said. "Look at those little creases on his wrists. He's positively chubby."

"That's what I've been telling you," chimed in Toby.

"He's the cutest baby I've ever seen," declared Zoe. "When will he be old enough to play?"

"Around six months," said Sara, causing everyone at the table to look at her in surprise. "What?" she responded defensively. "I took that baby-sitting course, remember?"

"I remember. I'm just surprised you do," said a familiar voice.

Lucy turned around and saw Elizabeth, city chic in tight black jeans, stilettos, and streaked hair. "I thought you were in Boston," she exclaimed, jumping up to hug her daughter.

"I took the bus. I couldn't miss brunch at the Queen Vic," Elizabeth said, taking the last seat. "I used to work here, remember? Today they're waiting on me!"

"Well, now that we're all here," announced Bill, "let's hit the buffet."

■ ■ ■ ■

It was really a moment to savor, thought Lucy when she returned with a plateful of favorite foods: fruit salad with melon and berries, eggs Benedict, smoked salmon, and a croissant. And that was just to start. The buffet featured a raw bar with shrimp and oysters, stuffed chicken breast, ham, roast beef sliced to order, vegetable medleys, and salads, plus a lavish tiered display of desserts, set up in the middle of the elegant dining room. But while the food was delicious, there was only so much a body could eat. It was spending time with her family, especially Elizabeth, whom she didn't see that often, and the new baby, that was most precious to her.

Seeing them like this, with clean faces and dressed in their best clothes and minding their manners, was priceless. She couldn't help but be proud of them. Toby, with his broad shoulders and easy smile; Elizabeth in her sophisticated clothes and city haircut; Sara, who had shed her baby fat and emerged as a graceful will-o'-the-wisp; and Zoe, with her sweet round face and big blue eyes. And they didn't just look good: they were good citizens. Toby was recognized by the other fishermen as a hard worker and a capable seaman, Elizabeth not only had top grades but had been chosen by her college to be a resident advisor, Sara was an honor student and cheerleader who also volunteered at the local animal shelter, and Zoe was the delight of her teachers and a keen member of the youth soccer team.

She looked across the table at Bill, who was about to eat an enormous piece of sausage, and smiled at him. She was a good mother, but she couldn't have done it without him.

"What are you smiling about?" he asked, spearing a piece of bacon with his fork.

"I'm just happy. It's really special to be here with you all," replied Lucy.

"I can't believe the baby is sleeping," said Molly. "I was afraid he'd scream his head off. This is special."

Toby made eye contact with his father and, receiving a nod, pulled two pink envelopes out of his jacket. "Dad and I wanted to make it even more special," he began, "so we got these for you."

Lucy opened the thick envelope, which was lined with glossy pink paper, and withdrew a card printed with raised letters: PURE BLISS. Opening it, she found a gift certificate entitling her to a facial, body wrap, massage, manicure, and pedicure at the fabulous new spa everybody was talking about that had recently opened at the ritzy Salt Aire Resort and Spa.

"You shouldn't have," she said. She was about to add that the gift was too expensive but bit her tongue just in time. This present, this Mother's Day, wasn't about her. It was for Molly, and she realized that her gift certificate came with a string attached: to make sure Molly got to the spa. "This will be fun, won't it, Molly? A whole day of pampering."

"I can't leave the baby for an entire day," Molly said, shaking her head.

"Sure you can," said Toby. "I'll take care of him."

Sara chimed in. "We'll help, too, won't we, Zoe?"

"I can't wait," agreed Zoe.

Molly shook her head. "You can't feed him. . . ."

"They can, if you pump in advance," said Lucy. "And you won't be gone all day, especially if we tell them to put us on the fast track."

"Well," Molly said, sighing, "it does sound fabulous."

"I can't wait. Let's book our appoint—," began Lucy, but she was interrupted in mid-sentence by a strident, complaining voice that cut through the hum of conversation and the tinkle of silverware to silence the entire room.

"This is unacceptable, simply unacceptable. When I made the reservation, I specifically requested the table in the corner with two windows."

Lucy recognized Barbara Hume, who was standing in the doorway with her husband, Bart, and her sixteen-year-old daughter, Ashley. Today, as usual, the family projected an image of perfection. Bart, actually Dr. Barton Higginson Hume, was a noted cardiac surgeon. Tall and reedy, he towered over his petite wife. Barbara, who preferred to be called Bar, "just like Mrs. Bush, the *first* Mrs. Bush," never seemed to have a single shellacked hair out of place. Today she was as trim as ever, in a pale green suit and bone pumps with matching bag. Ashley was standing behind her parents, and even though she was perfectly turned out in a pink, pleated miniskirt and matching jacket, she was slouching awkwardly, with her toes turned in.

"I demand to see Jasper," continued Bar, her voice growing even louder and more authoritative. Everyone in the room turned to watch as the inn's longtime maître d'

16

hurried over.

"Is there a problem?" he asked.

"I'll say there's a problem. I was promised that the corner table, that one with the two windows," said Bar, raising a perfectly manicured hand and pointing with her pink-tipped finger, "would be reserved for us."

Lucy also recognized the family occupying the table, the Nowaks, who were making a point of ignoring the fuss. At least Tina was. She was a large, sporty woman and was shoveling in forkfuls of food, intent on getting her money's worth out of the buffet. Her husband, Lenny, a slight, serious man with a mop of curly gray hair, who wore oversize tortoiseshell eyeglasses, was staring at his plate and pushing his food around with his fork, looking distinctly uncomfortable. In contrast, their sixteen-year-old daughter, Heather, was staring contemptuously at Bar, just as you might expect from a talented figure skater who competed regularly and wasn't afraid of a challenge.

"It's a family tradition," continued Bar in a voice that carried to the farthest corners of the room. "We come here every year for Mother's Day, and we always sit at that table."

Jasper cleared his voice and folded his

hands. "I am so sorry. There must have been some confusion. We have some new staff members from Ukraine. . . ."

"The person I spoke to was not Ukrainian. She spoke perfect English."

"I regret the mistake," continued Jasper, "but as you can see, the table is occupied. I will be happy to seat you someplace else."

"I did not reserve a table 'someplace else,' " snapped Bar. "I demand that you move those Nowaks from the table that should have been reserved for us and reseat them." Bar glared at Tina. "Frankly, I wouldn't be surprised if *somebody* hasn't done this on purpose, just to slight me."

If she was hoping to get a response from Tina, she was disappointed.

Bart, however, cleared his throat, perhaps signaling his wife to cease and desist. If he thought such a subtle hint would calm Bar, he was mistaken.

She snapped her head around to face him, eyes ablaze. "Darling," she began in a tone that was hardly loving, "perhaps you should slip the maître d' a little something so we can get the table we want."

At the Nowaks' table, Tina's face reddened, but she continued to concentrate on her food. Her husband, Lenny, looked as if he was ready to abandon ship and vacate the table. He half rose from his chair but, receiving a sharp glance from Tina, sat back down. Heather was smirking, evidently finding the entire episode just another example of parental foolishness.

Jasper assumed a pained expression. "That will not be necessary," he said. "Now, since it is impossible —"

"Nothing's impossible," declared Bar, eyes blazing. "Since you've gone to the trouble of importing all these Ukrainians, temporary workers, I presume, who will be returning to their native villages at the end of the summer?"

"Absolutely," said Jasper, with a nod. "They all have temporary work visas."

"You'd better see they do. The country's already got twelve million illegal aliens, you know, and we don't need any more. Especially since most of them don't even bother to learn English."

"We screen our temporary workers very carefully, and I can assure you they all speak English."

"Well, that's something. Now, why don't you put them to work and have them reseat *those* people" — she pointed at the Nowaks — "so we can have *our* table."

Jasper's professional veneer of patience was wearing thin. "We cannot disturb the other diners," he said. "I'll be happy to seat you at another table."

"Come along, Bar," said Bart, taking his wife by the elbow. "How about that table over there? It's by a window, too."

"But it's not the corner," replied Bar. "It's not *our* table."

Bart was firm. "It's a window, and I'm hungry."

"Oh, all right," Bar said, with a sigh, dramatically rolling her eyes. "I don't want to make a fuss."

"Right, Mom," muttered Ashley, sarcastically, as the group was ushered past the desired corner table.

Tina waited until Bar was behind her chair, and then she spoke to her husband. "Don't you think it was rude of Bar to make such a fuss?" she asked in a loud whisper. "Especially for someone who thinks she's the next Emily Post."

Bar pretended not to hear the comment but seemed to flinch slightly as she followed Jasper to the small window table adjacent to the Stones' large round one. Jasper made an elaborate show of pulling out chairs for Bar and Ashley and even placed napkins on their laps with a graceful flourish and snapped his fingers to attract the water boy's attention. He was filling their glasses when Bar took her revenge.

"You know," she began, placing her hand on her husband's arm and leaning toward him, speaking in a low tone that nevertheless carried across the room, "sometimes when I'm target shooting, I imagine Tina Nowak's face on the target." She giggled and smoothed her napkin. "It's a surefire way to get a bull's-eye."

CHAPTER TWO

"What's with that woman?" asked Elizabeth on the ride home. "Did you hear what she said?"

"I think the whole room heard it," said Lucy, who was feeling rather uncomfortable. She'd eaten too much and couldn't wait to get out of those control-top panty hose. And her thoughts had returned to Corinne Appleton's mother, a woman whose problems were real, in contrast to Bar Hume, who made them up. "I think she meant them to. She wanted to create a scene and shock people."

"But why?" persisted Elizabeth. "Why would she say a thing like that? It's like saying she wanted to shoot Mrs. Nowak. Why would she even think it? It's sick."

"It's the clash of the supermoms," explained Lucy. "Somebody ought to make a movie. They're always trying to outdo each other. It's a continuing drama, kind of like a soap opera. Everybody gets a kick out of it. Some people have even taken up sides, depending on their politics. Bar's a Republican, she's head of the town Republican committee, and Tina's a Democrat. She's head of the town Democratic committee. They actually do quite a bit of good for everybody as they try to outshine each other."

"It still sounds sick to me," said Elizabeth. "Especially when one starts talking about shooting the other."

"Nobody's going to shoot anybody," said Bill. "You've been living in Boston, after all. They're always shooting each other there. But it's different here in Tinker's Cove. Right, Lucy?"

Lucy didn't answer immediately. She was looking out the window at the round little harbor, where white boats bobbed on the still blue water. She was thinking about Corinne and what her parents must be going through, wondering if she was still alive. "Sometimes I think this thing between Bar and Tina goes too far, especially the way they push their daughters into competing with each other."

"What do you mean?" asked Elizabeth.

"They're tied for valedictorian," said Sara. "They have the same grade point averages, but Heather does take easier courses, because she has to spend so much time practicing her ice skating. She's a figure skater, she's won a lot of prizes, and she wants to go to Harvard."

"She's going to the regionals," said Lucy, who had written a story for the *Pennysaver.* "She has a good chance of placing high enough to go on to the nationals."

"Does the other one — what's her name? — skate, too?" asked Elizabeth.

"Ashley? No, she doesn't skate," said Sara. "Ashley's captain of the tennis team and the field hockey team, too. She takes the hardest courses she can. She even takes classes at the college. She wants to go to Harvard, too."

"Does she want to go, or does her mother want her to go?" asked Bill, making the turn onto Red Top Road.

"I think Mr. Berg wants her to go," said Sara, naming the high school principal.

"Getting a student into Harvard would be a feather in his cap," said Lucy. "Nobody's been accepted there since Richie Goodman, have they?"

"Not that it did him much good," said Bill. "What's he doing? Still in school, isn't he?"

"He's pursuing a doctorate in ancient

Greek ceramics or something like that," said Lucy, who was friends with his mother, Rachel. "But he's taking a break this semester to build houses in New Orleans for people who lost their homes in Hurricane Katrina."

"You sure don't need a Harvard degree to do that," said Bill.

"So how do these girls act at school?" asked Elizabeth. "Are they friends?"

"Yeah, pretty much," said Sara. "They both belong to the same clique, you know, the popular kids. They all sit together at lunch, and they're mean to everyone else."

"Oh, I'm so glad I'm out of high school," sighed Elizabeth.

"My friends don't like them very much," said Sara, with a shrug. "Even though they're the most popular, they're mean to each other, too. They're always saying nasty things about each other, even when they're ganging up on somebody else."

"I noticed they couldn't keep their eyes off of each other," said Elizabeth.

"Probably checking out their outfits," guessed Lucy.

"Maybe it's like Machiavelli said," mused Elizabeth.

"Who is Macaroni?" asked Zoe, joining the conversation.

"Machiavelli. He's a fifteenth-century Italian philosopher. He said you should keep your friends close, and your enemies closer."

Lucy nudged Bill. "And you were saying Chamberlain's too expensive. Look at the stuff she's learning."

"Well," muttered Bill, turning into the driveway, "let's see what sort of job she can get when she graduates."

Mother's Day was definitely over, thought Lucy, surveying the kitchen as she poured her first cup of coffee on Monday morning. The pan Bill had used to fry himself a couple of eggs was still on the stove, coated with grease and burned-on egg. One of the girls had slopped milk on the counter when she fixed herself a bowl of cereal, the table was covered with toast crumbs, and the dog had gotten into the garbage, scattering soggy tea bags, empty cans, and bits of empty food packages across the floor.

Lucy was reaching for the sponge when Elizabeth appeared and asked if she could do a load of wash before leaving for Boston.

"I don't think there's time," said Lucy. "I have to get to work by nine."

"But my bus isn't until eleven. Can't you come home and take me then?"

"I guess so," grumbled Lucy, thinking of her boss Ted's reaction. He'd been acting

26

like a bit of a Tartar lately, becoming a real stickler for punctuality and keeping a close eye on Lucy's time card. Unable to think of any other explanation, she'd chalked it up to male menopause.

Two and a half hours later, it went exactly as she had imagined. "Where the hell do you think you're going?" he demanded as she headed for the door, with her keys in hand.

Phyllis, the receptionist, who also handled classified ads and events listings, gave her a look. "The listings are especially heavy this week," she said.

"I have to take Elizabeth to the bus. I'll be back in a flash," promised Lucy.

"Make sure you are," warned Ted.

Lucy shrugged it off; she was already late, but she wondered what exactly he had in mind. Was he threatening to fire her?

When she got home, Lucy found Elizabeth dressed and waiting impatiently for her ride, the clean clothes packed in a duffel. The kitchen, which she had tidied before leaving for work, was once again a mess, with the stove and countertop filled with dirty pots and mixing bowls. The fruit basket, which she had filled on Saturday, was empty.

"I hope you don't mind. I made some food to take back. Healthy stuff, like brown rice salad and grilled vegetables and fresh fruit."

"No problem," said Lucy, a bit grudgingly but unwilling to end Elizabeth's brief visit with an argument. Now, of course, she'd have to stop at the grocery on her way home from work, something she hadn't been planning to do. Lucy sighed and grabbed the cooler Elizabeth was "borrowing" to carry the food back to Boston.

"I thought you'd be glad I won't be eating fast food," said Elizabeth, grabbing the duffel and following her mother out the door.

"Sorry. I'm just distracted," said Lucy, starting the car. That was a fancy cooler she'd snagged at an end-of-season sale last fall; she'd never be able to replace it for what she'd paid.

"Yeah, I'm worried about Sara, too," said Elizabeth, fastening her seat belt.

Lucy's head snapped around. "Why are you worried about Sara?"

"She was up half the night, text-messaging her friends."

This was news to Lucy. "What is she doing that for?"

"It's what kids do now. Instead of talking on the phone, like we used to do, they use

28

their cell phones to send text messages. That way nobody can overhear them. Nobody knows what they're saying. It's more private."

Lucy considered this as she turned out of the driveway. Come to think of it, the phone in the house hardly ever rang anymore. Thanks to the family plan, they all had cell phones, even Zoe. The days when the kids would scramble to get to the household phone whenever it rang were over; they knew it was only likely to be a telemarketer or one of their parents' friends.

"But why do they send these messages at night?" asked Lucy.

"Because that's when they're alone. There's nobody looking over their shoulders, nobody watching them, nobody noticing."

"Okay, I guess I understand that. There's nothing the matter with a few messages before she gets tired and turns the phone off."

Elizabeth turned and faced her mother. "Mom, they're not exactly telling each other to sleep tight."

"No?"

"No. They play these mind games with each other. They start fake rumors. They tear each other apart."

Lucy couldn't believe it. "Sara wouldn't do anything like that."

"Maybe not, but that doesn't mean her so-called friends aren't doing it to her. Last night I heard her crying under the covers."

"I'm amazed." Lucy braked at the stop sign. "I didn't know anything about this."

"I bet you don't know she has a page on myspace.com, either."

Lucy didn't know. "She does?"

"Yes. And you know that sexual predators prowl those sites all the time, looking for unhappy, vulnerable kids." Elizabeth sighed. "And believe me, that's most high school kids."

Alarm bells were beginning to ring in Lucy's head. Was this what had happened to Corinne? Had she met someone in a chat room, someone who seemed to understand her and appreciate her, but turned out to be some sort of sexual predator? "I'll have a little talk with her," she said, pulling up at the Quik-Stop, where the bus picked up passengers.

"Before you do that, I think you should do some research, okay? You need to know what you're up against." Elizabeth handed her a slip of paper. "This is how you can break into myspace.com."

"Thanks for telling me," said Lucy as Elizabeth climbed out of the car. "Have you got your bus ticket?"

"No, I didn't have enough cash for a round trip."

Lucy couldn't believe it. Just when she thought Elizabeth was all grown up, she'd go and do something stupid, like taking a trip without bringing along enough money. And now there wasn't time to go to the ATM. "How much do you need?" she asked, hoping she had enough cash in her wallet.

"A couple of twenties would do it, Mom."

Lucy handed them over, leaving herself with a couple of tattered singles.

"Thanks for everything, Mom." Then the bus pulled in, Lucy gave her daughter a quick hug, and she was gone, in a puff of diesel exhaust. But the concerns she'd shared with her mother about Sara lingered like heavy smog, clouding Lucy's mood.

When she got back to the office, Ted was gone and Phyllis was waiting for her return so she could go to lunch. "Now that I'm on this maintenance diet, I've got to eat every three hours, or else I get so hungry, I overeat," she explained, smoothing her gray sweater set over her flat tummy. "I get all shaky, you know, 'cause I don't have any reserves." She looked over her shoulder.

"And you know how Ted is these days. He threw out the sign with the little clock that said back in whatever minutes."

It was true. They were under strict orders to never, ever leave the office unattended during business hours.

"I'm sorry," said Lucy. "I had to get Elizabeth to the bus. It isn't as if she discussed her plans with me. It's always last minute with her."

"You're too soft on those kids. You let them walk all over you," said Phyllis, who never hesitated to give child-rearing advice, even though she'd never married and was childless.

Maybe she's right, thought Lucy, listening to the little tinkle of the bell on the door as it closed after Phyllis. She sat down at her desk and shrugged out of her Windbreaker, letting it slip down between the chair and her back. She started working on the listings, then impulsively switched to the Internet and went to myspace.com, where she followed Elizabeth's directions and called up Sara's page. It was a bit of a shock to see a photo of her daughter on her computer, but she had to admit it was a flattering picture. There were also several other pictures of her with friends, and most surprising, one with the family dog, Libby.

Although Sara volunteered regularly at the animal shelter, at home she tended to steer clear of the Lab, claiming she smelled bad. But here they were on MySpace, posed ear to ear and smiling, even Libby.

When it came to personal information, Lucy learned her daughter liked "pretty much all music," didn't watch much TV but was addicted to *Grey's Anatomy,* and didn't drink or smoke. So far, so good. She hoped to go to college and become a veterinarian. Even better. She admitted to being straight, but that was all. She wasn't looking for love on the Web. It all seemed pretty harmless. So what was Elizabeth making such a fuss about?

Just to be thorough, she typed in a couple of Sara's friends, with similar results. She even looked up Ashley Hume and Heather Nowak, again learning little more than that Ashley never missed *Survivor* and Heather loved Sudoku, before Ted marched in and she had to switch back to the listings.

Phyllis was right; there were a lot. Now that the weather was warming up, every club and organization in town seemed to be planning a yard sale or rummage sale or silent auction. It made Lucy wonder if there was some giant pool of unwanted items that were circulated from one event to another, from sale to sale, year after year. And if they weren't selling you old junk, they wanted to feed you ham and beans or barbecued chicken or roast beef. The VFW was even holding a pig roast. Those who still had some cash after the sales and dinners could see a show. The Tinker's Cove High School Players were selling advance tickets to their upcoming production of *Grease,* the Comedy Club was putting on *Sylvia,* and the Wentworth College Drama Club was presenting *Titus Andronicus.*

Just thinking about all this activity was tiring, and Lucy was glad when the clock finally read four thirty and she could leave.

"Any chance you could stay late tonight?" asked Ted. "We're swamped this week."

"I've got to pick up Sara," replied Lucy. "But I can come in early tomorrow morning."

"I suppose that's okay," he said, grumbling.

It was only a short drive over to the ball field behind the high school, where Lucy was supposed to pick up Sara. Today the boy's baseball team was playing archrival Gilead, and there was a lot of interest. Quite a crowd had gathered to watch the game, and she could hear groans as a Tinker's

Cove player struck out, ending the game with a loss. She stood by the gate as people left the field, exchanging greetings with many of them. As the crowd thinned, and there was no sign of Sara, she began asking if anyone had seen her.

"She was here," recalled Wilf Lundgren, the letter carrier. "I saw her with a couple of other girls."

"When was that?"

"Second, mebbe third inning. Bases were loaded, and that Gilead kid everybody's talking about hit one right over the fence. It was a grand slam." He sighed. "Gotta give it to the kid. He's a phenom."

"But you didn't see her after that?"

Wilf shook his head.

As Lucy followed the last of the stragglers to the parking lot, she checked her cell phone, just in case she'd missed a call. She hadn't. She clicked the phone shut, unpleasantly aware of a tightening in her chest. Darn it, she thought angrily, everybody was all sweetness and light on Mother's Day, but what about the rest of the year? Sara knew she was supposed to check in with her mother if she changed plans.

The thought stopped Lucy in her tracks. The truth was, Sara was very good about calling. What if something had happened that made calling impossible, like an accident?

No, if there had been an accident, she would have heard. There would have been sirens, at least.

The tightening feeling in her chest was getting worse, and now she was aware of a sinking feeling in her gut as Elizabeth's words came back to her. *Sexual predators prowl MySpace, looking for unhappy, vulnerable kids.* And Sara had been crying under the covers last night. Maybe she had a secret life on the Internet; maybe she had foolishly agreed to meet some weirdo at the game. Or somewhere else. She could already be miles from home, at the mercy of some serial killer who preyed on young girls. Lucy screwed her eyes shut. "Please, oh please don't let Sara be the next Corinne Appleton," she prayed. Opening her eyes, she realized she was all alone. Everybody was gone. She hurried to the car and drove home as fast as she could, trying to think what she should do. Call Bill? Call the police? She had decided to start with Sara's friends when she pulled into the driveway and hurried up the porch steps. When she opened the kitchen door, the first thing she saw was Sara, standing in front of the open refrigerator, looking for a snack.

She stood a moment, waiting for the pounding in her heart to slow down.

"There's nothing to eat," complained Sara, shutting the refrigerator door. "Not even a piece of fruit."

"Elizabeth took it." Lucy remembered she'd meant to stop at the grocery store, before she'd been distracted by Sara's disappearance. "Where were you? I was worried sick when I couldn't find you at the game!"

"Oh, sorry, Mom," said Sara, leaning casually against the refrigerator. "I got a ride home."

"Well, I wish you'd called and told me. I got so worried that I completely forgot we don't have anything for supper. Elizabeth cleaned us out." She thumped down in a chair, her purse in her lap. "And who gave you this ride, anyway? You're not supposed to accept rides from strangers."

Sara crossed her arms across her chest and hugged herself, a dreamy expression on her face. "It was Chad Mackenzie, Mom, the most popular boy in school!"

CHAPTER THREE

Sara was still giddy over her social triumph at breakfast the next morning. Instead of the usual moans and groans, she was positively bubbly as she poured herself a glass of orange juice.

"Would you like an egg? Some toast?" asked Lucy. She hadn't wanted to ruin Sara's mood last night by confronting her about the text-messaging, and now there wasn't time, but she hadn't forgotten the matter, either. She intended to bring it up when the time was right.

"No thanks," replied Sara, practically singing. "Just juice."

"You need more than that to get through the morning."

"I want to lose a few pounds."

"She wants to get skinny for Chad," offered Zoe in a singsong voice.

"That might be a mistake," said Lucy. "He probably likes you the way you are. If he didn't, he wouldn't have bothered to give you a ride."

"He probably felt sorry for her, standing there all alone like a little lost lemon drop, waiting for her mother to come," declared Zoe.

Lucy gave her youngest a sharp look.

"I was just joking, Mom," Zoe added.

"I guess I will have a yogurt," decided Sara. "It's got calcium, and that's supposed to help you lose weight." She smiled dreamily. "You know what Renee and Sassie think? They think Chad might ask me to the prom."

"Oh, my," said Lucy, who wasn't sure how she felt about her freshman daughter going to the prom. She was about to add, "Don't get your hopes up," but managed to bite her tongue before uttering the fatal phrase. There was no sense spoiling Sara's happiness, however brief it might be. Especially since her change of mood had infected the whole house; even the dog was wagging her tail more enthusiastically than usual when the girls ran down the drive to catch the bus.

Lucy, too, felt especially chipper as she drove to work. She was the first to admit it wasn't easy to have a daughter in high school. It brought back her own memories of adolescent insecurity, to the point that she suffered sympathy pains whenever Sara's feelings got hurt, and shared in her joy when she scored a coup. It was a real roller coaster, but today, at least, spirits were high.

Until, that is, she got to work. There was a very different vibe at the *Pennysaver*, where Phyllis was sniffling and dabbing at her eyes, and Ted was grimly poring through old issues from the morgue.

"What's going on?" she asked.

Phyllis reached for a tissue and blew her nose. "They found Corinne Appleton's body," she said.

Lucy's happy mood instantly evaporated as she waited to hear the rest of the story.

"What they think is her body," corrected Ted. "There's only a few bones."

"And a piece of a bra," added Phyllis.

"A hiker made the discovery," said Ted. "Out near Shiloh."

"Her poor parents," said Lucy. They had been on TV so often, pleading for their daughter's return, that Lucy felt as if she knew them. She could picture them clearly, the tall, quiet, whiskered father and the frizzy-haired, emotional little mother. Lucy couldn't help identifying with them, especially when Joanne Appleton appeared wearing the same quilted jacket that Lucy owned.

"It's tough," said Ted, closing one of the big books of bound *Pennysavers* with a thud. "There's a press conference at ten in Shiloh. I'll cover that. Lucy, I want you to write some background. We covered it pretty extensively, so it's all here, in last summer's papers."

"Right," said Lucy, wishing she could wiggle out of it somehow. It was hard enough writing about it the first time, and she didn't want to go over it all again.

"At least now her parents know for sure what happened," said Phyllis. "They'll have closure."

"Whatever that is," muttered Lucy, studying the photo of Corinne that had appeared on the front page of every newspaper in the state, maybe even in the whole country. It was one of those stories that the media, and the public, couldn't get enough of. She was only sixteen, a pretty girl with a round face and long dark hair. She was smiling in the photo, and there was a dimple in each cheek. Like most towns in the area, Shiloh offered a recreation program for kids during the summer school vacation, which included games, field trips, arts and crafts, and even swimming and boating lessons. Corinne had been a counselor for the eight- to ten-year-olds. It was her first job.

The rec program started at nine in the morning and ran until noon, but Corinne's mother had dropped her off earlier, before eight thirty, because that was when she had to be at her job at a bank. "It seemed safe," she was quoted as saying. "A park, right in the center of town. This is her home, after all. Everybody knew her and she knew everybody. If a girl isn't safe in Shiloh, she isn't safe anywhere."

Nobody had seen anything out of the ordinary. One moment Corinne was there, sitting on the bandstand, reading a book, and the next time anybody noticed, she was gone. Nobody had thought anything of it. Maybe she'd gone to get a cup of coffee or a bottle of sunscreen; maybe she'd gone inside the supply shed to get balls and bats for a planned baseball game. But when everybody assembled for the morning exercises, when they raised the flag and sang "This Land Is Your Land," she wasn't there. The recreation director had noted her absence and assigned someone else to take her place. He'd meant to call and see if she was sick, but nine-year-old Tommy Branson tripped on a rock and fell, breaking a tooth, and what with calling his mother and getting him off to the dentist, the director had forgot all about Corinne until her mother called sometime after noon, wondering why she hadn't shown up at the bank, as she always did, so her mother could give her a ride home on her lunch break. By then she'd been missing for nearly four hours, time for an abductor to have taken her more than two hundred miles away.

The story hit a nerve; it was all people in the region talked about for months. Many volunteered for search parties and spent long, hot hours trudging through the buggy woods; others put up posters on trees and utility poles. The Shiloh selectmen debated discontinuing the recreation program, fearful it was putting the town's children in jeopardy. In the end, a police officer was assigned to patrol the park while the program was in session. The summer ended without further incident. No further abductions were attempted, and Corinne remained missing. Some people even speculated that perhaps the Appletons weren't as nice as everybody thought, and perhaps Corinne had run away because of problems at home.

"Now," wrote Lucy, "ten months after her disappearance last July, the longstanding mystery of Corinne Appleton's fate appears to have been solved." She typed slowly, weighing her words, trying to chart a course between a cold, factual account and a maudlin appeal to readers' emotions. When she finally finished, she was exhausted.

"I think I'll take a little walk before I tackle the listings," she told Phyllis, but she hadn't got out the door before Ted returned.

"What did they say?" demanded Phyllis. "Is it really Corinne?"

Ted nodded, taking off his jacket and hanging it on the coatrack. "Her mother identified the bra. It was pink with flowers. She said she'd washed it many times."

Lucy thought of the many times she'd handled her own girls' clothing, taking the clean bras and underpants and shirts and jeans out of the dryer and folding them, making neat piles topped with their rolled-up socks, which she placed on their beds for them to put away in their dresser drawers.

"There wasn't actually much of her body left," said Ted. "Just a few bones. They think the body might actually be elsewhere, maybe even buried, and animals dispersed the bones, but there's enough that they can do DNA testing."

"What's that mean? That animals dispersed the bones? Did they eat her?" asked Phyllis, never one to mince words.

Ted sighed, reluctant to answer. "There are tooth marks on the bones."

"Is there anything that indicates how she died?" asked Lucy.

"Not so far," said Ted, "but forensic teams are going to comb the area where the bones were found. They're confident that they'll find more evidence."

He left it there; he didn't say the obvious. It now seemed clear that Corinne had not voluntarily run away; someone had abducted her and killed her. And the evil predator who had done it was still at large.

That night, Lucy and Bill sat down with Sara and Zoe for a little talk about safety.

"We don't want you to end up like poor Corinne," said Lucy. "You can't ever get in a car with a stranger."

"Or even somebody you know, unless you have our permission," added Bill.

"That's crazy," complained Sara. "Do I have to call every time one of my friends offers me a ride?"

"No. You know what I mean. People we know but don't really know. Like bag men from the supermarket . . ."

"Are the bag men kidnappers?" asked Zoe.

"Probably not. We don't know. That's the point," said Bill. "Just because you recognize somebody doesn't mean you really know them."

"Like the fathers, or even mothers, of your classmates," said Lucy. "If Dad and I don't know them, you need to be cautious and check with us."

"But if you don't know them, how will you know if they're bad?" Zoe asked.

"That's not the issue," said Bill. "We're not making judgments about people. We just want to know where you are and who you're with."

Sara didn't like this at all. "So I have to tell you everything I do, everywhere I go?" she protested angrily. "That's crazy. I won't have any privacy at all."

"We're not trying to control your life, or keep you from your friends. We just want you to be safe," said Lucy, frustrated that this was turning out to be so difficult. "Poor Corinne is nothing but a pile of bones now. I couldn't stand and your dad couldn't stand, for that to happen to you, to either of you."

Sara's face was set in denial. "That couldn't happen to me. Corinne was dumb. It said in the paper that she was playing around in Internet chat rooms and that she probably made a date to meet someone."

"That was never proved," said Lucy. "As

far as I know, she was just waiting for the rec program to start. She had a job. I don't think she'd make a date for a morning she was supposed to work." She paused. "But since you brought it up, I know you're no stranger to the Internet yourself."

Bill's eyebrows shot up. "What?"

"So I have a page on MySpace. So what?" Sara demanded defensively. "Everybody does it. Everybody has one."

"That's enough of that," said Bill, his jaw set. "We're going to look at this page right now. Let's go." He marched over to the computer in a corner of the family room. "Show me."

Zoe was fidgeting nervously with her armful of friendship bracelets. "What do you think happened to her, Mom?"

Lucy had done plenty of research; she knew how these things happened. "I think some very bad person tricked her with a fake story, like her mom was sick or had an accident, or there was an injured dog that needed to get to a vet fast, something like that. He told her to get in the car, that would be the fastest way, and she fell for it, thinking she was needed, that she was helping."

"And then he killed her?" asked Zoe.

"Probably a lot more than that," said Sara,

47

earning a warning look from her mother.

"We want to believe everyone in the world is good, but that's just not the case," said Lucy.

"Like Osama bin Laden," said Zoe.

"Exactly," said Bill, who was leaning over Sara's shoulder, staring at the monitor. "Only some bad guys don't go around in funny clothes, like Osama, and we haven't seen their photos on TV. So if somebody seems to be acting oddly to you, or asks you to do something you're not sure you should, you should say no and get someplace safe as fast as you can."

Seeing that Zoe's fidgeting was becoming frantic and she looked as if she was going to cry, Lucy put an arm around her shoulder and hugged her. "You don't need to be afraid. Chances are this will never happen to you. But we want you to know what to do if it does, okay?"

Zoe nodded bravely. "Okay."

"Well, this MySpace thing looks okay," said Bill, speaking slowly and straightening up. "But both of you girls know that you must never, ever under any circumstances agree to meet somebody who has contacted you on the Internet, right?"

Both girls nodded.

"And I do think there are better uses for

the computer, like for schoolwork," he continued. "I think you both ought to get started on your homework."

"I've got to call Chad," said Sara, standing up and smoothing her jeans. "He asked me to the prom, you know."

"Did you say yes?" asked Zoe, clapping her hands together.

"I told him I'd think about it," said Sara.

Zoe was shocked. "Aren't you going to say yes?"

"Of course, I am, but not right away. I don't want to seem too eager." She looked at her parents. "And I know I need permission from you."

Lucy's and Bill's eyes met. Who knew their daughter was such a femme fatale?

"Everybody thought he was going with Ashley," said Zoe.

"He broke up with her," said Sara, looking smug. "Just like he broke up with Heather last year. Those girls are getting old."

"Old? They're sixteen," said Bill.

Sara corrected him. "Almost seventeen."

"Positively ancient," said Lucy, sarcastically.

"That's right. They're ancient history. They're almost seniors. Nobody dates seniors," Sara noted.

"Why not?" asked Lucy.

"Like I said, they're old. Boys, even seniors, like younger girls, like freshmen," Sara explained. "It looks like me and my friends are going to be the new popular kids."

Zoe's eyebrows shot up. "You?"

Sara rolled her eyes. "What's so strange about that? We're cheerleaders. We're cute. Justin Crane asked Renee to the prom, and Will Worthington gave Sassie a ride home today. I bet he'll ask her, too."

"What about Tommy?" asked Zoe, referring to a neighbor boy, also a freshman, who had shown some interest in Sara.

"He's nice," said Sara, "but you have to be a senior to buy tickets to the prom." She got up. "Well, I've got to call Chad. What shall I tell him? Can I go?"

Lucy's first instinct was to say no. Sara was too young and inexperienced to go out with a senior, especially to something as significant as the prom. She knew full well that many kids considered the evening incomplete unless it included sex and alcohol. But she also knew that she was probably alone in this. Despite his recent show of fatherly discipline, Bill was a notoriously soft touch where his daughters were concerned.

"What do you say, Dad?" demanded Sara.

Lucy caught his eye and gave her head a tiny shake. He answered with an apologetic half smile. "As long as we can set some ground rules," he said.

"Thank you, thank you!" exclaimed Sara, giving him a big hug before dashing off to make the call. Zoe followed close on her heels, whooping.

When they were gone, Lucy turned to Bill. "Are you crazy?"

"Lucy, she's growing up. She's pretty. She's smart. Boys are going to be attracted to her. You can't stop it. It's like holding back the tide."

"I know," admitted Lucy. "But I don't like her attitude." Lucy remembered the pudgy little Sara who used to eat too much and was constantly teased about it by her older sister, Elizabeth. "What happened to our little Sara?"

"She's a big girl now," said Bill.

"Chad is three years older than she is," said Lucy. "He's a senior, and he can drive. That opens up a whole new can of worms. Drinking and driving and sex."

Bill's jaw dropped, and he swallowed hard. "Have you had that little talk with her?"

"Of course, I have," she snapped. "I don't think a little talk provides much protection."

Bill stood up, clenching his fists. "If he lays a hand on her, I'll kill him."

"Whoa, Papa. How come you didn't think about this before you gave her permission to go to the prom?"

Bill's face was blank. "I didn't think . . ."

"Well, it's too late now. All we can do is hope for the best." She patted his hand. "Look, Chad's an honor student, a star athlete. All indications are he's a good kid. And we have to have some faith in Sara. After all, we brought her up to be responsible."

"Like I said, he messes with my little girl, I'll kill him," repeated Bill.

Lucy watched as he marched out of the room. A minute or two later, she heard the lawn mower start up. He was going to work off his anxiety by mowing the lawn. She felt the need for some distraction herself, so she grabbed the remote and sat back on the couch, put her feet up on the coffee table, and clicked on the TV, just in time to see Corinne Appleton's parents giving a statement to the press. It was the last thing she wanted to see, but she couldn't turn away.

"The day we've dreaded for so long has come," said Bob Appleton. "We know now that Corinne will never return. All we can do now is hope that the terrible person who did this to her will be caught and punished. We want to thank all the law enforcement officials who have worked so tirelessly to solve this case, and we know they won't rest until justice is done. Thank you."

Lucy watched, wiping her eyes, as Joanne Appleton stepped up to the microphone. "I just want to add," she said, brushing her long, curly hair out of her eyes, "that Corinne was a lovely, smart girl, a sensible girl, who made a foolish mistake. Tonight I hope you'll all hold your daughters close and tell them how much you love them."

At that the grieving woman's voice broke, and she turned away from the cameras. On the couch, Lucy was biting her lip, choking back sobs. Concerned, Libby began licking her face.

"What about closure?" called a reporter. "Can you get on with your lives now?"

Bob Appleton had aged since last summer, his cheeks had sunken, and he spoke slowly, as if forming words were painful. "Frankly," he said, "I wish they'd never found those bones. Finding those bones took away hope, and I would rather have died hoping that Corinne was alive."

Then he turned and put his arm around his wife's shaking shoulders and led her back inside their white clapboard house with a porch and a steep peaked roof, a house that looked remarkably similar to the Stones' old farmhouse.

CHAPTER FOUR

Lucy was still thinking about Corinne Appleton when she got to work on Wednesday morning. She couldn't understand why the police hadn't been able to identify her abductor. These were small towns, after all, where everybody supposedly knew everybody. It seemed incomprehensible that such a monster could go unrecognized for so long. So when Ted asked her to interview Rick Johnson, the hiker who had found Corinne's remains, she was eager to talk to him. But when she finally got him on the phone, there was less than an hour to go before deadline. It wasn't that he was particularly elusive. It just happened that there were thirty-one R, Rick, and Richard Johnsons in the phone book.

"Boy, you're a hard guy to find," she began, after identifying herself. "Have a lot of reporters been calling?"

"No. You're the first," he said. "I'm the

last one in the book 'cause my wife's name is Zephira."

Lucy smiled, pleased to have a scoop. "Well, I really appreciate your talking to me. Can you tell me how you happened to find the bones?"

"Well, I'm a real nature enthusiast," he began. "I like to hike and I'm a bit of a bird-watcher and this is the season for May warblers. I was hoping to add a few to my life list. So I wasn't looking at the ground. I was following this old logging road that I know and looking up in the trees when I tripped on something. I looked down and saw it was a bone. Looked like a rib to me. I figured it was from a deer or maybe even a moose, but then I noticed this little bit of cloth kinda stuck on it, and then I knew it wasn't from no deer, and when I looked around, I saw there were some more bones. I had my cell phone, o' course, so I called the state police. It took a while for 'em to find me. They had to kind of triangulate off a fire tower, Bald Mountain, and a dirt road. The road's still in pretty good shape, and it's been a dry spring, so it wasn't too muddy."

"Did you suspect it was Corinne's bones? Is that why you called the state police?"

"Nope. I didn't put two and two together.

To tell the truth, I wasn't sure exactly what town I was in, and I didn't want to call the wrong department. The lines get kinda blurry out there in the woods, and I was kinda distracted by a black-throated blue. I mean, I was close enough to touch it. Amazing." He paused. "But the cops, the staties, they said it might be this Corinne who disappeared last summer."

"How did that make you feel?"

"Well, they were congratulating me and telling me what a hero I was for calling, but I didn't see it that way. I've got daughters myself, and I'd sure hate for them to end up like that. I guess the crime scene guys found more, but all I saw, really, was a couple of bones. They were pretty brown. You might o' thought they was sticks, but I've been in the woods enough to know what bones look like. Mostly though, this time o' year, you see deer, the weak, old ones that didn't make it through the winter. It was kind of a shock to see that little bit of cloth with the pink flowers. To tell the truth, I haven't had a good night's sleep since. I keep worrying about my girls."

"I have daughters, too," said Lucy. "I know what you mean." She was typing as she spoke and apologized for keeping him waiting. "Just one more question. Where exactly did you find the bones? Was it far in the woods?"

"Nah. As it turned out, it wasn't far at all, but I didn't realize it, because I started in from the Gilead side. You know the town of Shiloh?"

"Sure."

"Well, you know Main Street, and then there's that side road by the church that runs back to the town highways department? Behind the library?"

"Yup."

"Well, the pavement ends at the highway department, but the road continues on up into the hills there. They keep it clear 'cause o' forest fires, you know? It's no problem getting a car in there."

Lucy was stunned. "So she was there, all that time, only a mile or two from home?"

"Sad, isn't it?"

"It's tragic," said Lucy. "I wonder why all those search parties didn't find her sooner?"

Rick's voice dropped to a whisper. "I wondered that myself, but the cops said she might not have been there when everybody was searching. She might've been held captive somewhere, something like that, maybe for months, even."

Lucy had heard a lot of theories about Corinne's mysterious disappearance, but this was the worst. "I didn't think of that. That's horrible."

"Yeah," Rick replied. "That's why I can't sleep."

It didn't take Lucy long to write up the interview after she'd thanked Rick for his time and hung up, and she shipped it to Ted a minute or two before the old Regulator clock on the wall read twelve o'clock. Her work done, she headed for the IGA to do her grocery shopping, but her mind was on Corinne as she wheeled the cart around the aisles. She simply couldn't believe — she didn't want to believe — that the poor girl's body had been lying there all along, only a short distance from home.

What a bitter pill for Corinne's parents, she thought, pausing in front of a display of detergent bottles. They were on sale, a two-for-one introductory special, and Lucy debated whether she should risk trying the new brand. It was supposed to be good for the environment, but would it clean Bill's work clothes? Why was she even wasting time like this, she wondered, unless it was to escape thinking about Corinne? She quickly loaded two of the biodegradable jugs into her cart and rounded the corner, heading for the checkout. She was just beginning to unload the cart onto the conveyer belt when she noticed Bar and Tina meeting at the newspaper rack.

Watching, she couldn't help thinking it was really a clash of cultures, East meets West, Right meets Left, something like that. As usual, Bar's short blond hair was stiff with hair spray, and she was wearing a pastel knit suit with a knee-length skirt and pumps. Tina was her exact opposite, with long, flowing hair, naturally streaked with gray. She was wearing loosely cut slacks and a flowing jacket that practically screamed natural fiber, topped with an oversize hand-crafted necklace. The one thing they did have in common was the phony smile each woman had pasted on her face as they both reached for the last copy of the *Boston Globe*. Appropriately enough, Tina had the left side, and Bar the right. Neither one seemed inclined to let go.

"It's my paper," said Bar. "I was here first."

"No, you weren't. I was first," said Tina, tossing her long hair over her shoulder. "Besides, I'm a subscriber, but the driver missed me this morning."

"That's not my problem," said Bar, speaking in a low voice and enunciating clearly. "I always buy my copy here. I'm a regular customer, so it's mine by rights."

"That's so typical," fumed Tina. "You think you can have everything you want, including my table at brunch!"

"Admit it. You took that table just to spite me."

Tina shook her head. "Can't you let it go? I had nothing to do with it. Jasper just happened to seat us there."

"I don't believe it for a minute."

"Why? Is he on your payroll or something?" Tina smiled. "If you want to know what I think, I think Jasper seated us there because he wanted to have an attractive, happy family sitting at such a visible table."

Bar didn't like that at all. "That is so rude, but I should know better than to expect anything else from you," she said, keeping her voice low but claiming the high ground. "There's no reason to get personal. It's not nice. And for your information, you and your happy family didn't look all that happy to me!"

Lucy kept on unloading her cart. She didn't dare meet the cashier's eyes, or she knew she'd start laughing.

"I see you bought that new Mother Earth detergent," said Dot, beginning to scan the groceries.

"I thought I'd give it a try," said Lucy, who was keeping an eye on the dispute at the newspaper rack.

"We were until you came and spoiled it all," declared Tina, raising her voice and attempting to yank the *Globe* out of Bar's hands. "And not just for us, but for everyone there. Do you think they really wanted to hear you carrying on like that?"

"I was just standing up for what's right," said Bar, with an indulgent smile. "I was promised that table. But this is the last time we'll be patronizing that place. Bart was saying the food isn't as good as it used to be and the service —"

"Oh, so now Bart is a gourmand?" sneered Tina. "How come I'm always seeing his car outside that joint — what's it called? — the Rainbow Inn."

"I think you should apologize immediately," said Bar, giving the paper a sharp tug. "My husband is a highly respected cardiac surgeon."

Tina's face was red, and her eyes were bulging. "He's a pill-pushing Medicaid cheat with a wandering eye, that's what he is, and everybody knows it," she screamed. "Now give me my paper!"

"You're a bully, and I won't give in to bullies," hissed Bar. "Let go of *my* paper!"

"No, you let go!"

"No, you!"

"I think I better intervene, before they come to blows," said Dot. She marched over and snatched the paper, ending their tug-of-war. "I know this is the last *Globe*. Maybe we can toss a coin or something. Meanwhile, let me point out there are plenty of other papers, including the *New York Times* and *Wall Street Journal*."

"I want the *Globe*," said Bar.

"And she has to get what she wants," snarled Tina. "Even if it belongs to someone else."

"Actually, this *Globe* belongs to Mr. Marzetti," said Dot, naming the owner of the store. "But what do you say we split it, for free? There's six sections. You can each have three."

"I get City and Region," they both said simultaneously.

"Now, that's a problem," said Dot, folding the paper and tucking it under her arm. "I think you better both take the *Herald*. No charge."

"Oh, all right. give her the *Globe*," exclaimed Bar, throwing her hands up. "At least the *Herald* supports our president, and I won't have to deal with the *Globe*'s liberal bias just to find out what happened to that poor girl."

"It's not biased," insisted Tina, snatching

the paper from Dot. "It's the *Herald* that's biased."

Bar's eyes were blazing, and she was about to reply when Lucy interrupted. "I think you should read the *Pennysaver*," she said, unable to resist a plug. "Tomorrow's issue has an exclusive story about the Corinne Appleton case."

They both tuned in and looked at her. Then they both burst into laughter and went on their separate ways, shaking their heads.

"What's so funny?" asked Lucy when Dot returned to the register. "We do a good job at the *Pennysaver.* I've got the only interview with the guy who found the bones."

"I never miss an issue," said Dot, hitting the TOTAL button. "That'll be one-oh-three fifty-seven."

Libby greeted Lucy enthusiastically when she arrived home with the groceries, but despite her Labrador grin and wagging tail, most of her attention was focused on the bags of food. She gave each one a thorough sniffing, especially those containing meat.

"Down, down," ordered Lucy as she struggled to hoist several heavy bags onto the counter. It was only when she tossed a handful of dog biscuits on the floor that

Libby turned her attention away from the bag containing lamb chops, on sale for $5.99 a pound. Now that the family was smaller, Lucy could afford an occasional splurge.

When Lucy finished putting everything away, she made herself a peanut butter and jelly sandwich and took it to the kitchen table, along with a glass of milk. She sat there, staring out the window at the woods beyond the backyard, chewing thoughtfully.

This time of year she liked to walk in the woods, looking for wildflowers. They came in quick succession, beginning with lush green carpets of skunk cabbage in damp places and, tucked away in sheltered nooks, jack-in-the-pulpits. She knew where the trillium bloomed every year, and she often found bloodroot, foamflowers, and dogtooth violets. There were also survivors from long-vanished farms: lilacs and apple trees, patches of lily of the valley and, come summer, day lilies. But now that Corinne's bones had been found in the woods, she wasn't quite so keen to go hunting for wildflowers. It was silly. Shiloh was miles away, and there was little chance she would come upon anything more gruesome than a pile of feathers or a tuft of fur remaining from a hawk's dinner, but she didn't want to chance it. And, anyway, she sighed, getting up to put her plate and glass in the dishwasher, she'd be thinking of Corinne the whole time, thinking of her sweet, young body left exposed in the woods, where scavengers, like raccoons, coyotes, and crows, even pets, like cats and dogs, could gnaw on her.

Just thinking about the evil person who would do such a thing, who would harm a defenseless young girl, made her angry, and she made good use of her emotions, scrubbing away dirt and grime in the kitchen and bathrooms, and thoroughly vacuuming the family-room carpet. She was just putting her cleaning tools away when Libby's bark announced the arrival of the school bus.

She opened the door to let Libby out to greet Zoe and was surprised to see that Sara had taken the bus home, too. This was surprising because she knew Sara was planning to stay at school to watch Chad play baseball. She automatically reached to feel Sara's forehead when she came into the kitchen.

"Don't you feel good?" she asked. "Are you coming down with something?"

"I'm fine, Mom," said Sara.

"I thought you were staying for the game."

"I changed my mind."

Her tone was defensive, and Lucy cast a questioning look at Zoe, who just shrugged her shoulders.

Mentally, Lucy ran through the possibilities. A bad grade? A scolding from a teacher? A fight with Renee or Sassie? Chad with another girl? "Would you like a snack? I got some nice strawberries. . . ."

"I'm not hungry," said Sara, heading for the stairs and climbing them slowly, as if it were an effort.

"What's going on?" Lucy asked Zoe, who had pulled the box of berries out of the fridge and was sitting down at the table with them, dipping them into the sugar bowl before popping them in her mouth.

"I dunno, Mom," she answered, her mouth full.

"Don't talk with your mouth full, and let's put some of that sugar in a little dish so you don't spoil all the sugar in the sugar bowl."

"Oh, sorry, Mom."

"She didn't say anything?" asked Lucy.

"Nope."

"Was she alone?"

"No." Zoe put a berry in her mouth and chewed slowly and thoroughly. Lucy thought she'd scream, waiting for her to swallow. "She was with Chad."

"Really? How did they seem? Were they

fighting?"

"No." Another berry, another wait. "He kissed her."

Not exactly what Lucy wanted to hear. "He did? Right there in front of the school?"

"A little kiss. Not gross."

"Is that what upset her?"

Zoe shrugged, and Lucy headed up the stairs and tapped on Sara's door. When there was no answer, but she heard muffled sobs, Lucy went in. She found Sara face-down on her bed, with her face buried in her pillow. She sat down on the bed and placed her hand on Sara's back. "Want to tell me about it?"

"No."

"I think you should. You'll feel better."

"I'll never feel better. I want to die."

Alarmed, Lucy grabbed her shoulder and rolled her over so she could see her face. "Don't say things like that."

"It's how I feel," said Sara, tears streaming down her face.

"No boy is worth this. There'll be another, and another. Believe me."

"It's not Chad."

"Well, what is it then?"

"It's Heather and Ashley. They took a cell phone picture of me changing into my gym clothes and sent it to the entire football team!"

CHAPTER FIVE

The one bright spot that Lucy could count on in her week was the Thursday morning breakfast with her friends. The weekly get-together with Pam, Rachel, and Sue at Jake's Donut Shack had been a tradition for years now, adopted when their children got older and the four friends realized they weren't seeing as much of each other as they used to when they constantly met at school and sports events. The four decided they needed to set a time to get together, not only to stay in touch and gossip, but to offer support and sympathy when life became difficult.

Lucy had the most rigid schedule, but she was free on Thursdays until the eleven o'clock news budget meeting at the *Pennysaver*. Pam, who was married to Lucy's boss, Ted Stillings, taught dance at Winchester College, the liberal arts college on the outskirts of town. Rachel Goodman, married to attorney Bob Goodman, worked a couple of hours a day providing home care to the town's oldest resident, Miss Julia Ward Howe Tilley; and Sue Finch was part owner of a thriving child-care center, Little Prodigies. She filled in as a teacher when needed, but her primary role was administrative: developing curriculum, training teachers, and meeting with parents. They all made the breakfast a priority; it was the first thing they inked in their calendars every week. This week Lucy was really looking forward to sharing her troubles and getting some encouragement from her friends.

The others had already gathered at their usual table in the back corner when Lucy arrived.

"Oh, good," said Pam, signaling to the waitress. "Now we can order."

Lucy felt a stab of disappointment; she'd expected a warmer welcome. "What? No hello? How are you?" asked Lucy.

"Sorry. It's just that I'm in a bit of a hurry," said Pam, turning to the waitress. "I'll have my usual two eggs, sunny-side up, toast, and OJ."

"Okay," said Norine, with a shrug. "Regulars for the rest of you?"

"I think I'll try one of those sunshine muffins," said Rachel, abandoning her usual healthy bowl of oatmeal with skim milk.

"Taking a walk on the wild side?" commented Norine, writing it down on her pad.

"Hash and eggs for me," said Lucy.

"And just —," began Sue.

"Black coffee for you," said Norine, rolling her eyes and finishing the sentence for her.

Lucy was about to ask Pam why she was in a hurry this morning when Rachel began one of her lectures on good nutrition. "You should eat more," she was saying to Sue. "And you girls should switch to egg-white omelets," she added, speaking to Lucy and Pam. "They're much better for you."

"You should talk," protested Sue. "What happened to that bowl of heart-healthy oatmeal? Do you know how much sugar is in those muffins?"

"I do," said Rachel, somewhat shamefaced, "and I want it. To tell the truth, I need some comfort food. I keep thinking about that poor girl's bones. I can't stand thinking that she was lying out there, all alone, just a little way from home."

"I guess we could all use a little boost this morning," agreed Pam. "It's too, too sad."

"I feel so bad for her parents," said Lucy.

"Those searchers couldn't have done a very good job," said Sue.

"I don't know how they could have missed her," agreed Pam.

"Maybe she wasn't there when the search parties were out," said Lucy as Norine set her plate in front of her. Suddenly, the greasy hash and eggs and the toast slathered with butter didn't look quite so appetizing.

"You mean she could've been held captive?" asked Rachel, shuddering as she broke her muffin in two. "That's even worse."

"Or I suppose he could've moved the body, too," said Pam. "Maybe he waited, kept her in the freezer or something, until things died down."

"What creeps me out is thinking that whoever did this probably lives around here," said Sue, sipping her coffee. "They're supposed to notify the schools whenever a registered sex offender moves into the neighborhood, but I've seen the list, and I don't think this guy is on it."

"I think you're right. That was one of the first things the police did," said Lucy. "They went down the list and questioned them all."

"This may have been a first timer," said Rachel, who was a psych major in college. "They usually start peeping and stalking and gradually work up to killing their victims."

"Why do we think it's a man?" asked Pam, and all three looked at her.

"Isn't it always?" asked Lucy. "Women have other ways of acting out."

"Like those female teachers who fall in love with their students," Sue said as she flicked an imaginary piece of lint off the sleeve of her tweed jacket with a perfectly manicured finger.

"What do they see in those kids?" asked Pam, whose son, Tim, was now in graduate school. "Their sneakers alone . . ."

"The underwear!" added Rachel, whose grown son Richie was building houses in New Orleans. "No deodorant is strong enough!"

"Those women are certifiable," declared Lucy. "But there aren't very many of them, thank goodness. It seems to me the real danger in high school is the other students, especially the girls."

"What do you mean?" asked Pam.

Encouraged, Lucy began her tale of woe. "Well, Sara got asked to the prom by Chad Mackenzie, and now Ashley and Heather have started a hate campaign against her. It's outrageous. They took a photo of her changing for gym and sent it to the boys on

74

the football team."

"What a mean thing to do," clucked Rachel. "She wasn't naked, was she?"

"No, no," said Lucy. "She had on a sports bra and a pair of underpants."

"That's more than she was wearing last summer, when she was running around town in that bikini," said Sue.

"I know," admitted Lucy, who didn't like to be reminded of this particular escapade. "But in her defense, she really had no idea she was causing such a sensation. But this is different, you know. She feels betrayed."

"I don't think any of us would willingly go back to high school," said Sue. "It was a real low point in my life."

"It doesn't have to be," said Pam, biting into a piece of toast. "Don't forget, she is going to the prom with Chad Mackenzie. That must be some consolation."

"I can't say I'm surprised," said Rachel. "This sort of thing is pretty typical adolescent behavior."

"And just look at their mothers," said Sue, rolling her eyes.

Lucy took a bite of hash, then pushed her plate away. Since she wasn't getting the sympathy she'd hoped for, she might as well pass along a juicy bit of gossip. "I saw the most ridiculous thing yesterday. Bar and

Tina were actually fighting over the last copy of the *Boston Globe.* Dot Kirwan had to break it up before they came to blows over a seventy-five-cent newspaper."

"What kind of example is that for those girls?" asked Sue, clicking her tongue.

"A terrible example," said Rachel. "This feud of theirs is getting out of control. Did you hear about what happened at the Mother's Day brunch at the Queen Vic?"

"I haven't heard," said Sue. "What happened?"

"I was there," said Lucy, going on eagerly to recount the incident.

"Isn't that just like Bar?" commented Sue when Lucy had finished her description. "She does think she's always right and everybody else is wrong."

"Tina's no peach," muttered Rachel. "She was behind that Elder Services investigation. She thought I was helping Miss T so I could get her money!"

"Well, it worked out for the best," said Pam, patting her hand. "Now you're an official home health aide, and they pay you."

"But I never wanted to get paid," said Rachel. "And now I have to get CPR and first aid certification every year, and I have to go to all these inane workshops. All because that Tina's a big buttinsky."

76

"She does have a big butt," commented Sue, causing them all to laugh.

"Oh, I don't know," said Pam. "I kind of like her. She's loud and brassy, sure, but she's comfortable with herself, and that's an achievement for any woman. And her heart's in the right place. She does a lot of good for others."

"Even if they don't want it," said Rachel, smiling. "At least Bar minds her own business."

"Not exactly," said Sue, and they all turned to hear what she had to say. "Last year Ashley was helping out at the preschool — some sort of career internship program they have at the high school now — and she told her mother we had a book about a kid who has two mothers. Lesbians, you know, but that's never mentioned in the story. It's a cute little book, and it has all kinds of families. Big families, small families, kids being raised by grandparents, you know."

They all nodded.

"Well, Bar raised a huge stink over it, got a bunch of parents to threaten to pull their kids out unless we got rid of the book."

"How come I never heard about this?" asked Lucy, unhappy at missing an important story.

"Because the last thing we wanted was

publicity," said Sue, with a shrug. "We gave her the book, and I imagine she burned it."

"You caved?" exclaimed Pam.

"That's awful!" added Rachel.

"It was a business decision," said Sue. "I am not like Tina. I have better things to do than fight with Bar."

Phyllis was opening the mail when Lucy got to the office. She still dyed her hair bright orange and polished her nails in wild colors, but Lucy thought she looked older since she'd lost so much weight. Her cheeks had lost their roundness, and her chin sagged, but she often said she had more energy and felt younger than she had in years. Lucy wondered if it was true, or if she was trying to convince herself the weight loss had been a good idea.

"What's new with the girls?" she asked, slitting open an envelope.

"Not much. We talked about Corinne Appleton."

"You and everybody else," said Phyllis. "We got three letters to the editor about her."

"What do they say?"

"Gun nuts. If she'd only had a gun, she would have been able to defend herself."

"She was sixteen," said Lucy. "Do they

really want sixteen-year-olds running around with guns?"

"They want everybody to have guns," said Phyllis. "Issue them at birth. Give 'em a rattle in one hand and a shotgun in the other."

"By the way, where's Ted?"

"Said he'd be a bit late. Has a meeting at the bank."

Lucy's investigative mind began to make connections, remembering Pam's comment that she couldn't linger over breakfast. What were they up to? She knew a lot of small newspapers were being bought by giant news conglomerates. Was Ted ready to cash in?

"Might as well start on the listings," said Phyllis, interrupting her train of thought.

Ted arrived about half an hour later, marching straight to Phyllis's counter and plucking a copy of the paper off the pile that was sitting there. His first look at the new issue was always rather tense as he looked for typos they had missed. Lucy and Phyllis watched anxiously as he hung up his jacket and settled down at his desk.

"Looks good," he said, scanning the front page. "I put your interview with the bird guy right on page one."

"I noticed," said Lucy, watching as he

flipped through the pages.

"Any irate phone calls?" he asked Phyllis.

"No. It's been quiet," said Phyllis.

"Well, good," said Ted, folding the paper and setting it in front of him. Lucy and Phyllis each let out a sigh of relief. "Let's get started on next week. Lucy, I've got an idea."

Lucy groaned inwardly, putting on an eager smile. "What is it?"

"You know the prom's coming. . . ."

"Do I ever," said Lucy, with a sigh.

"Some parents are planning one of those after-prom parties, where they have all sorts of fun activities and prizes to keep the kids from driving around and getting drunk and killing themselves."

"Do kids actually go to these things?" asked Phyllis. "I thought the whole point of the prom was to get drunk and lose your virginity."

Lucy and Ted both looked at her in surprise.

"What's gotten into you?" asked Lucy. "Did you eat a cookie?"

"Two actually," admitted Phyllis. "You have no idea how good a chocolate chip cookie tastes if you haven't had one in a year."

"As I understand it, there'll be cookies at

the after-prom party, but no booze and no sex. Good, clean fun," said Ted, with a shrug. "I admit it, in my day, nobody would have been caught dead at a thing like that, but times are different. Last year's party was a big success, and they're hoping this year will be even better."

"So you want me to write a puff piece about it?" asked Lucy.

"Yes, I do. I've received a special request from the organizers."

"Who are?"

"Barbara Hume and Tina Nowak. They're cochairs," said Ted.

Lucy couldn't believe it. "You're sending me into the cross fire? Those women hate each other."

"Maybe so, but they seem to have put their differences aside in this worthy cause. They sent me a very nice letter, and they both signed it." He flourished a piece of flowery notepaper.

"Okay," said Lucy, doubtfully. "I'll go, but only if you equip me with body armor."

"I'm sure that won't be necessary," said Ted, consulting his calendar. "Now, there's a finance committee meeting this week, also planning board, and historical commission. I'll let you off easy, Lucy. You can have the planning board, and I'll take the others."

"Oh, thanks," said Lucy, anticipating a boring evening. At least Bar and Tina were bound to be interesting.

Setting up a meeting was no problem. As it happened, gushed Tina, the two were planning to meet that very afternoon, at her house. They'd be thrilled if Lucy would join them.

Lucy wasn't exactly thrilled, but she was curious when she arrived at Tina's ecologically designed "green" house, with its grass-covered roof and solar panels. She was standing on the front stoop, looking up at the waving sea of green, when Bar joined her.

"Amazing what some people will do, isn't it?" she asked, jabbing the doorbell with her trigger finger. She had apparently come straight from the shooting range and was still wearing her ammo vest over stretchy beige pants and turtleneck. She must have been wearing ear protectors, but they hadn't disturbed her hair, which sat on her head like a blond helmet.

"Come in, come in," sang Tina, opening the door for them. "I've got mochaccinos for everyone."

"Just water for me," said Bar as they trooped down the hall to the kitchen.

"I'd love a mochaccino," said Lucy, trying to get a peek at the living and dining rooms as she followed the others, but only getting a glimpse of kilim rugs and plant-filled windows. The kitchen was enormous, with a natural wood floor, polished concrete countertops and open shelving, instead of cabinets, that displayed a large collection of hand-thrown pottery. There were no windows in this part of the house, which was underground, but lighting created a warm, cozy feeling.

Lucy and Bar climbed onto stools at the center island, and Tina set their drinks in front of them. "Anything else I can get you ladies?"

Bar took a sip of water and grimaced. "Don't you have bottled water? I can't abide this stuff from the tap."

"I stopped buying it, and you should, too," lectured Tina. "The bottles are becoming a problem, filling up landfills. . . ."

"That's ridiculous," said Bar, pushing the glass away.

"This is delicious," said Lucy, taking a sip of her frothy drink. "So, tell me about the party."

"Well," began Bar, "I'm sure you're aware that there have been some tragic auto accidents following area high school proms in recent years."

"Not to mention other risky behaviors," added Tina.

"So last year a group of parents decided to do something about it," said Bar. "We formed a committee and put on an after-prom party. Some of us were doubtful it would attract the kids, but we threw in some really attractive prizes, like skateboards, iPods, even a brand-new used car donated by the Ford dealership, and it turned out to be quite a success."

"You said 'brand-new used car,' " said Tina, pointedly. "That's an oxymoron."

Lucy wondered if things were going to start to get ugly, but Bar just smiled condescendingly. "You know what I meant," she said, with a shrug.

Tina wasn't satisfied. "No. I don't know what a brand-new used car is, and nobody else does, either."

Lucy jumped in, eager to avoid another confrontation. She could sense the animosity the two women had for each other and was beginning to feel rather tense. "I'll just put in used car," she said. "What are the prizes this year?"

"They're fantastic. A trip to Cancún for spring break, ski-lift tickets, a Jet Ski, mountain bikes . . . It goes on and on," said

Tina, handing her a list.

"Nobody leaves without prizes," said Bar. "They all get goodie bags with fast-food coupons, all sorts of cute stuff."

"I really think those coupons are a bad idea," said Tina. "It would be better to give them wholesome energy bars, or gift certificates to the whole foods store."

Bar sighed. "McDonald's and Burger King gave us coupons. The people at the health food store gave us a twenty-dollar contribution, and they grumbled about that."

"I suppose their profit margin is slim," said Tina.

"I happen to know the owner, Inez, spent two weeks at Canyon Ranch last winter," replied Bar. "Do you have any idea how expensive that is?"

Tina decided to change the subject. "And we have live entertainment   the Claws are going to play — and no kid is going to want to miss it. I know my daughter, Heather, is really excited about going."

"My daughter, too," said Bar, turning to Lucy. "This will be Ashley's third prom. She's had a date every year since she was a freshman."

"My daughter Sara is going, too. She's only a freshman, but Chad Mackenzie asked her," said Lucy, unable to resist the temptation of bragging about her daughter's popularity.

Both women turned and fixed Lucy in their sights.

"Chad Mackenzie?" asked Tina, narrowing her eyes.

"I thought Chad was taking Ashley," said Bar, twitching her trigger finger. "I mean, I just assumed it when he broke up with Heather."

"Since when did they break up?" demanded Tina. "Heather never said a word about it. It was my understanding he was taking her."

Lucy was beginning to realize she'd made a big mistake and wished she could take back her boast. "Maybe he has three dates," she said, trying to make a joke.

"I don't think so," said Bar, speaking between clenched teeth. "You know what this means, don't you?"

"It means Heather is not going to be prom queen," said Tina, her voice bitter with disappointment.

"And neither is Ashley," said Bar, looking stunned.

"They're both lovely," protested Lucy. "They have a better chance than most of the girls."

"Not anymore," said Bar. "Chad will definitely be king."

"He's the most popular boy in the school," agreed Tina. "And chances are that his date will be queen."

Lucy was stunned. Sara? Prom queen? She was hardly able to wrap her mind around the idea when Bar pounced. "I'm sure you'll want to share in her triumph," she said, wrenching her mouth into something between a smile and a grimace. "Don't you want to see her in her crown?"

"I think you're getting a little ahead of yourselves here. Besides, parents don't go to the prom," said Lucy.

You could almost see the wheels turning in Tina's head. "But you could come to the after-prom party. We need lots of parent volunteers to help out."

"I guess I can help," said Lucy, thinking it would be worth losing a night's sleep to see Sara reign as prom queen.

"Oh, good," said Bar, making a note. "I'll just put you down as head of the recruitment subcommittee. I know we can count on you to deliver at least four volunteers."

"Uh, I wasn't . . . ," began Lucy, shaking her head.

"I know you'll do a great job," said Tina, smiling brightly. "Another mochaccino?"

Lucy declined, dropping her notebook into her bag and standing up. She felt as if she'd had a narrow escape and wanted to get out while she still could.

That night, Lucy and Sara went to the Galleria to look at prom dresses. As they drove along the interstate, Lucy was tempted to ask Sara about the laxatives and diet pills Zoe had reported seeing, but decided against it. This was supposed to be a happy mother-daughter experience, and she didn't want to spoil it. And besides, she'd seen no sign that Sara was using them.

"We don't have to make a final decision tonight," said Lucy, excited to see what the store was offering. "Let's just see what's available, what looks good."

"Okay," agreed Sara. "How much can I spend?"

"I saw some nice dresses advertised in the paper for under a hundred dollars."

"Probably a come-on," grumbled Sara. "I want to look good. This is my first prom, and I want to make a good impression. And remember, I'll need shoes and probably a strapless bra, and I'll have to get my hair done, and then there's tanning. I know it's not good for you, but everybody does it, and I don't want to look like a ghost. . . ."

"Maybe we can get some of that instant tanning cream instead," suggested Lucy.

"That stuff makes you look orange," said Sara.

Turning off at the exit, Lucy braced herself for a struggle. "Let's pick some up and give it a try," she said, turning off the ignition and grabbing her purse.

Once inside the big department store at the Galleria, they had no trouble finding the prom dresses, which spilled out of the juniors department in a colorful array of lace and chiffon and even crinoline.

"I don't want to look like Scarlett O'Hara," commented Sara, taking in a full-skirted number in hot pink.

"It is kind of overwhelming," said Lucy, starting with the nearest rack. She flipped through one garishly colored evening gown after another, marveling at what fashion designers actually thought teenage girls should wear.

"I think I'll try this on," said Sara, holding up a sparkly pale pink sheath and eyeing it doubtfully. "It's ninety-nine ninety-nine."

"It's pretty," said Lucy, stopping to study a shimmery, ice blue, bias-cut satin dress. It was clearly in a different class from the other, fussy dresses. She grabbed it off the rack and followed Sara into the dressing room. "Try this one, too," she said.

'Okay," said Sara, disappearing behind the louvered door. Lucy leaned against the wall, waiting. Why couldn't they put a chair or two in here? she wondered as she pressed her aching back against the wall.

"The pink didn't fit," said Sara, stepping out in the blue dress.

Lucy almost gasped in surprise. It fit perfectly, the satin snugly accentuating Sara's trim figure. The color perfectly complemented her rosy coloring. With her hair simply styled, she would look like a modern-day Carole Lombard.

"Do you know how much this costs?" whispered Sara.

Lucy looked at the tag, which read $299.99. A penny short of three hundred dollars. She'd never spent that much on a dress for herself, much less for one of her daughters.

"No matter," said Lucy, throwing thrift to the wind, picturing Sara in her prom queen crown. "In that dress, you'll be the prettiest girl at the prom!"

CHAPTER SIX

Lucy was tired on Friday morning. It had been a later than usual night, thanks to the shopping trip to the Galleria, but definitely worthwhile, even if it meant she'd have to struggle to get through the day. At least that was what Lucy told herself as she poured herself a third cup of coffee from the pot in the office. The dress had been a real find — though expensive — and it suited Sara perfectly, magically mixing sweet youth with a soupçon of sophistication.

"Soupçon of sophistication? What on earth does that mean?" demanded Phyllis when Lucy tried to describe the dress to her.

"Well, it looks classy, not slutty," said Lucy. "It shows off her figure, but it's not too low cut or anything like that. It's really lovely."

Phyllis humphed. "This is the beginning," she warned. "You better watch out she doesn't turn out like Elfrida. She got pregnant at her prom."

Lucy considered Elfrida, Phyllis's notorious cousin. With six children and numerous marriages on her résumé, she was hardly a role model for any teenage girl.

"Well, I don't think Sara is ready for that," said Lucy. "And now those boozy after-prom parties in motel rooms are a thing of the past. The party Bar and Tina are organizing is going to be very well chaperoned, because I'm in charge of recruiting chaperones. In fact, I'll be there myself."

"Lucky you," said Phyllis, turning the charm on for the letter carrier, Wilf Lundgren, who handed her a thick bundle of letters fastened with an industrial-strength rubber band. "Thanks so much," she said, giving him a big smile.

"It's always a pleasure to see you," he said, smiling back. "You really brighten my morning."

Phyllis simpered and batted her eyelashes. "I bet you say that to all the girls," she said.

"No, not at all," said Wilf, taking a deep breath and plunging in. "You're special, Phyllis. What say we get together for a bite after work?"

"That would be lovely," said Phyllis, with a big smile. "What time?"

"I'll come by your house at six. Is that okay?"

"I'll be looking forward to it," she replied, with a twinkle in her eye.

Lucy was amazed. "Since when have you been sweet on Wilf?" she asked when he had gone.

"I've had my eye on him for a while," said Phyllis, sorting through the letters. "His wife died about six months ago, and he gave her such a beautiful funeral — the casket was covered with tons and tons of pale pink roses — and at the time I thought he must be a real romantic at heart."

Lucy remembered how Wilf had come to her rescue years ago, when she was new to town and the lights had gone out in their house. Wilf had gone down into the cellar and fixed the problem. "There is something of the knight in shining armor about him," said Lucy.

"Exactly," said Phyllis, handing her a press release accompanied by a photo. "Lookee here. This is one lady who doesn't look like she needs a knight to rescue her."

It was a photo of Bar Hume, dressed in shooting gear, complete with goggles and ear protectors and an ammo vest, pointing a handgun at a target in the shape of a person. A cluster of holes indicated that if the target had been an actual person, it would be a very dead person, having been shot in the heart numerous times.

"Goodness," said Lucy, wondering if Bar had imagined the target was Tina Nowak, just as she'd said at the brunch. "It says here she's been chosen Gun Woman of the Year by the Maine Gun and Rifle Association."

"Well, goody for her," said Phyllis, taking a good look at the photo. "All I've got to say is it's a good thing she's married, because that getup is not the sort of thing men find attractive."

Lucy considered. "I dunno. Bart seems pretty keen on her. Maybe he has a thing for women in goggles."

"Goggles, a big maybe. Guns, no. Absolutely not. Call me old fashioned, but I don't think there's a place for guns in a romantic relationship. Roses, yes. Chocolates, yes. Champagne, yes. Guns, no."

"I think that's good advice. If everybody followed it, we'd have a lot less domestic violence to report in the paper."

"What's this?" demanded Ted, who had yanked the door open and set the little bell jangling. He was practically salivating. "A tragic domestic assault?"

"Not yet," said Lucy, showing him the photo. "But I think we should all keep our heads down now that we have the Gun Woman of the Year living right here in town."

Ted grimaced, studying the photo. "Better be careful what you write about her in that story," he warned Lucy. "Meanwhile, I'll put in an order for that body armor you requested."

"It won't be necessary," said Lucy, waving the press release at him. "It says right here that Bar 'exemplifies the highest standards of gun safety and responsible gun ownership, while exercising her constitutional right to bear arms to defend herself, her family, and her country.' "

"I'm sure she does," said Ted, "but I'm not going to go knocking on her door at night, that's for sure."

"I guess that's the point," said Lucy, who was on the second page of the press release. "She's letting everyone know she's no helpless victim like poor Corinne. She's even planning to teach a self-defense class for women in the adult ed program."

"Oh, that reminds me," said Ted, seating himself at his desk and switching on his computer. "There's a lot of talk that the cops are following a hot lead in the Appleton case. Maybe you can call some of your contacts and find out what's happening?"

"I'll try," said Lucy, "but don't expect much."

"I've got confidence in you, Lucy," insisted Ted. "If anybody can get them to talk, it's you."

Lucy suspected Ted was being sarcastic. She didn't have especially good relationships with the local cops. On the contrary, she knew they regarded her as a thorn in their sides, always poking her nose in where it wasn't wanted. She decided to begin with Officer Barney Culpepper, the one cop who was an old friend, dating back to the days when their boys were Cub Scouts and they both served on the Pack Committee. But since those days were long gone, she didn't expect much. Nowadays their relationship was primarily professional. Barney was the community outreach officer and spent a lot of time speaking to clubs and school groups about safety. No matter if it was stranger danger at Halloween, warnings about fireworks on the Fourth of July, or the rules of the road for bicyclists, Barney was your man. What he didn't know much about was the status of ongoing investigations of serious crimes.

"Gee, Lucy, I wish I could help," he said, "but right now I've been focusing on reminding people not to leave valuable stuff in unlocked cars. Now that the weather's warmer, they'll go off and leave video cameras, laptops, cell phones, even purses, right there for anybody to take. And then they're all upset when they get back to the car and find they've been robbed."

People sure can be foolish, thought Lucy, who knew she was guilty of leaving things in her car. She never thought to lock it, either. In fact, hardly anyone in town even bothered to lock their houses.

"They should at least put valuables in the trunk, where they're out of sight," he continued.

"Right," said Lucy, who drove a Subaru station wagon with no trunk at all. The car did have a sliding screen, but she never used it, figuring it would tip off a thief to the presence of something valuable. "I wasn't looking for specifics, you know. I just wondered if you might've heard anything at the station that might mean they're close to making an arrest or something."

"Nope. Not a word, not a peep. The boys from the state are running this now, and they don't tell us anything."

Lucy knew this was a continuing source of irritation to the town cops. She hoped her sympathetic tone would loosen his lips. "Sometimes they use you, though, don't they? To check on the status of sex offenders, stuff like that?"

"Oh, sure, they use us, but they never tell us why," he grumbled.

"Yeah, well, they want all the credit for themselves," said Lucy, laying it on thick.

"You know it," agreed Barney.

"So have they requested anything like that lately?" she persisted.

"Not from me. The only thing I got was a memo they sent to all the community outreach officers in the state to remind kids of stranger danger now that summer is coming and school will be out."

"But there haven't been any incidents since Corinne, have there?"

"No, that's the problem. These guys are like time bombs. They can handle the urges for a while, but the pressure builds, and sooner or later they have to do it again. Mebbe you could put something about that in the paper, Lucy. It's just a suggestion. I don't mean to tell you your business, but people need to be aware that he's still out there."

Not exactly encouraging news, thought Lucy, thinking of Sara and Zoe. "I'll do that, Barney. Thanks for the tip."

"No problem," he said, managing to sound as if he'd given her the scoop of the century.

"What was the tip?" demanded Ted, eagerly.

"Hold the presses," said Lucy. "People need to be aware that Corinne's abductor is still at large, and should therefore instruct their kids to exercise caution when dealing with strangers."

"Oh," said Ted, disappointed. "Is that all?"

"Not quite. We also need to remind people not to leave valuable articles unattended in their automobiles."

"I suppose hurricane season is just around the corner, too," said Ted, referring to the police department's annual advisory.

"He forgot to mention that," said Lucy, considering her options. She didn't think it was worth bothering the police chief, who was new at the job and had his hands full managing the department. The state police officer in charge of the investigation, Detective Horowitz, was an old acquaintance of Lucy's but not in a good way. She doubted he would even take her call. No, it was time to go to the top. She decided to head to the IGA.

Dot Kirwan, the head cashier, smiled as Lucy approached with a bag of premixed salad. "Don't you love that stuff?" she asked. "If you ask me, it's the best thing they've come up with since sliced bread."

"It's worth the price not to have to wash and dry and tear the lettuce," said Lucy. The store was practically empty, and Dot was free to chat, which was the purpose of her visit. Lucy knew that Dot's numerous offspring worked in the police and fire departments, and her oldest son had recently been promoted to chief.

"It's a real time-saver, isn't it?" said Dot, scanning the bag. "That'll be two-fifty. It's on sale. Two for five dollars."

"Great," said Lucy, opening her purse. "You know, now that the weather's warming up and the kids are outside more, well, I can't help but think about what happened to that poor Corinne Appleton, and I'm so worried about my girls."

"It's a worry, isn't it?" agreed Dot, giving her change.

"Have you heard anything at all? Are they close to making an arrest?"

"Funny you should ask," said Dot, settling her bottom against the cash drawer. "I've been over at the chief's a lot because Bonnie had knee surgery. . . ."

"Oh, I'm sorry to hear that," said Lucy.

"Just minor, that arthur-scope-ic kind, where they just make a little hole and poke something in there to fix the problem, but she's got quite an active brood there with the three boys, and she's supposed to stay off her feet. Well, anyway, that's beside the point, but the chief was talking at dinner last night, and he said he wouldn't be surprised at all if they were on to something, the state police, that is, because he hasn't heard a word from them lately."

"Oh, really," said Lucy, wondering where this was going.

"Really," repeated Dot. "He says that when they clam up, it means something is up."

"Oh," said Lucy, getting her drift. "Loose lips sink ships, is that it?"

"You got it. They don't want anything to mess up whatever it is they're up to."

"Well, let's hope he's right," said Lucy, taking her bag. "I know we'll all rest a lot easier if they catch this guy."

"Amen," said Dot.

Back at the *Pennysaver,* Lucy reported what Dot had told her and settled down to write the story about the after-prom party. As she listened to her tape recorder, she was struck by the level of hostility the two women had exhibited at the same time they'd been pretending to cooperate on a worthy project.

What Lucy found most disturbing, however, was the way they'd spoken about each other's daughter. There had been real venom in Bar's voice when she'd asserted that although Heather and Ashley had the same grade point averages, Heather didn't take the challenging advanced placement courses that Ashley did. Tina hadn't responded directly, not even when Bar had praised Heather's figure skating but also expressed concern that Heather looked as if she'd gained a few pounds and that might throw her off. She'd waited until Lucy asked if any students were involved in planning the party to mention that "of course, Heather is very involved. She's created a text-message campaign to publicize the event, but Ashley is too busy with the tennis team and her AP courses to help." When Bar began to bristle, she'd added, "Of course, I understand poor Ashley really has to struggle to keep her grades up."

It struck Lucy that the sparring was almost a reflex: they simply couldn't stop making digs at each other. And they'd gone after her, too, when they'd realized Sara posed a threat to their daughters' popularity. It was no wonder that the girls themselves were using similar tactics; they'd learned from masters.

She was still thinking about the rivalry between the two women when she stopped on the way home to pick up a pizza for dinner. Pizza was a Friday night tradition, providing a quick supper before the evening's activities. Sara was going to the movies with Sassie and Renee, Zoe was sleeping over at Sadie's house, and Lucy and Bill were going to baby-sit so Molly and Toby could enjoy a quiet dinner together.

Lucy was carrying the pizza into the house when Bill pulled into the driveway. She waited to greet him, watching as he walked around to the passenger side and pulled out a big bag with a discount store logo.

"What have you got there?" she asked.

"Toys for Patrick. For tonight."

"But he's only eight weeks old."

"You're never too young to start," said Bill, pulling out a huge baseball mitt.

Lucy shook her head, laughing. "He could fit in that mitt."

"He'll love it," said Bill, putting it back in the bag. "It's even got a Red Sox logo."

But when the grandparents took over and Bill switched on the TV to watch the game, sitting in the rocking chair with the baby in his lap, just like he used to do with his own kids, he discovered Patrick was not a Red

Sox fan. All Patrick wanted to do was cry.

Bill finally gave up and handed the tiny tyke over to Lucy, who tried everything she could think of. She changed his diaper, she offered him a bottle of his mother's milk, she offered him a bottle of water, she tried a pacifier, and she even took him for a little drive, hoping the motion of the car would soothe him. Nothing did, until he finally fell asleep around ten o'clock.

"I'm exhausted," she told Bill as she collapsed on the couch. "I don't know how his poor parents do it."

"Me, too," said Bill. "I could hardly hear the game with all that crying."

CHAPTER SEVEN

The birds were singing, the tulips were up, and the lilacs were budding. It was a gorgeous Saturday morning in May. The sun was already warm at eight o'clock as Lucy strolled about in the garden, checking the progress of the seeds she had planted. The peas were poking through the soil, as were the lettuce, spinach, and radish seedlings. It wouldn't be long before they would be eating homegrown salads and vegetables.

Lucy and Molly had scheduled spa appointments at ten o'clock, so Lucy decided to put the time to good use by trying to recruit her Prudence Path neighbors to help out at the after-prom party. Frankie, whose daughter Renee was also a freshman, was sitting on her deck, with a cup of coffee. She waved to Lucy, inviting her over.

"Isn't this weather glorious?" she asked. She was seated on a cushioned chaise lounge, with her legs bare to the sun.

"Would you like some coffee?"

"No, thanks," said Lucy. "Don't get up. You look so comfortable."

"I don't mind, really," she said, popping up. "I'm actually a bit cold and could use a sweater. I'm trying to tan my legs, just a little bit."

"Well, if you're going inside, anyway . . ."

"Back in a mo'."

Lucy sat down on a rattan café chair and admired Frankie's deck, which looked like a bit of Provence transported to Maine. Not that Lucy had actually been to Provence, but she'd seen photos of Provence-style decor in magazines. Frankie had put out plenty of terracotta planters filled with impatiens and geraniums, and she'd added lots of pillows covered in classic red, yellow, green, and blue prints. There was even a market umbrella over the table.

"I love what you've done with the deck," said Lucy when Frankie returned with a steaming mug. "The pillows are beautiful."

Frankie smiled. "I got them in France last summer." Lucy knew that Frankie, actually Francoise LaChance, visited her French relatives every summer, along with her daughter Renee.

"I'm jealous," said Lucy, taking a sip of the delicious coffee. "I'd love to visit

France."

"I don't know if I'm going to be able to go this summer," she said, with a shrug. "The airfare has gotten so expensive. No deals in summertime."

"Is Renee disappointed?"

"No, she'd rather stay here with her friends."

"Is she going to the prom?" asked Lucy.

"With a football player. Justin Crane." Frankie took a sip of coffee. "I wasn't happy about it, but Frankie brought him home to meet me, and he seems okay."

"Well, that's one reason I wanted to talk to you," said Lucy. "I'm looking for volunteers for the after-prom party. Maybe you could help out?"

Frankie's eyes widened. "Are you doing that? Staying up all night?"

"I figured I'd be up, anyway, worrying, so I might as well be keeping an eye on Sara."

"I know the party is well intentioned, but I'm a little reluctant to invade Renee's territory, if you know what I mean. I think I'd like to talk to her about it before I make a commitment."

"Fair enough," said Lucy, reluctantly getting to her feet. "I wish I could stay here all day. It's so peaceful."

"Me, too, but I have to go sell a house."

"Good luck," said Lucy.

She crossed the street, heading for the Westwoods' house to talk to Willie, also the mother of a freshman, Sassie. Like Sara and Renee, Sassie was a cheerleader. Her little brother, Chip, was shooting baskets in the driveway, accompanied by the family's dogs, an Irish setter and a Lab.

"Hi, Chip," said Lucy as the dogs approached, tails wagging. "Is your mom home?"

"Hi, Mrs. Stone. I'll get her for you," he said, disappearing inside, leaving the dogs to keep her company. Lucy smiled, hearing his voice as he went from room to room, yelling "Mom!"

"Sorry about that," said Willie, coming around the side of the house. "I was cleaning the rabbit hutch. Come on in." She opened the door, and when the dogs attempted to slide through, she stopped them with a look. She was a tall, sturdy sort who spent every spare moment riding her horse.

Lucy followed Willie into the kitchen, where she set about washing her hands. When she finished, she asked Lucy if she wanted some coffee.

"No, thanks," said Lucy, who was feeling rather jangly from Frankie's strong brew. "I know you're busy, and I won't keep you.

I'm recruiting volunteers for the after-prom party, and I wondered if you'd help out."

"I would, but Sassie's not going."

"I'm surprised," said Lucy. "I heard that Will Worthington was going to ask her."

"Oh, he did, but her father won't let her go." Willie raised her eyebrows.

"Wow," said Lucy, impressed at Scratch's willpower, moral stamina, and parental fortitude. "How's Sassie taking it?"

"Not well," admitted Willie. "The atmosphere in this house is like Berlin, before they took the wall down. Scratch and I are the evil East German guards. Sassie is the rebellious freedom fighter determined to get over the wall."

Lucy chuckled. "Well, good luck with that. You can't possibly chaperone. You'll have your hands full here at Checkpoint Charlie."

"You can say that again," said Willie.

Lucy was only too well aware that she was zero for two as she headed down the street, toward Molly and Toby's house, and was searching her brain for possible chaperones when she saw Tommy Stanton coming toward her on his bicycle. Like the girls, Tommy was also a freshman, but he still looked boyish, with skinny shoulders, long legs, and big hands and feet.

Lucy smiled and greeted him but was surprised when he braked and stopped, one foot on the ground and one propped on a pedal.

"Hi, Mrs. Stone," he said.

"Beautiful day, isn't it?" she replied.

"Sure is, but I won't get to enjoy it. I've got an all-day rehearsal. I'm in the chorus for *Grease.*"

Lucy knew he was in the drama club, an organization that Sara insisted was only for losers. "It'll all be worth it when you take your bows," she said.

"Yeah, it's actually a lot of fun," he admitted. "The kids in the club are really nice." He stood awkwardly, looking down at his foot, then raised his head. "I dunno. Maybe I shouldn't say anything, but do you know that Sara is going steady with Chad Mackenzie?"

"He's taking her to the prom," said Lucy.

Tommy's cheeks were reddening, and his Adam's apple was bobbing in his skinny neck. "Well, I just think you ought to know that he's no good. He gets the girls to think he's in love with them and gets as much," — here Tommy's face grew scarlet — "as much as he can from them, and then he dumps them and starts with another. He's already worked his way through most of the

110

senior, junior, and sophomore classes!"

"I know you're Sara's good friend," said Lucy.

Tommy was once again studying his shoe. "Well, you know, she's real nice, and I don't want her to get hurt."

"Oh, she'll get hurt," said Lucy. "We all do sooner or later. But I'm not worried about Chad. I suspect Sara knows what she's doing."

Tommy looked surprised. "You do?"

Lucy smiled. "I think she's flattered by the attention and looking forward to the prom, but I think that's about as far as it goes."

Tommy perked up. "You mean she doesn't like him?"

"Sure, she likes him, but I don't think they have much in common. I wouldn't be surprised if she got bored with him pretty soon."

"You think?" Tommy was ecstatic.

"That's what I think," said Lucy, watching as Tommy sped away on his bike. Tommy was skinny and gawky now, but if he took after his older brother, Preston, he'd be extremely good looking in a year or two, and then all the girls would be chasing him. She was smiling as she tapped on Molly and Toby's kitchen door.

"C'mon in," said Molly, looking up with bleary eyes from the kitchen table, where she was sitting with a cup of decaf. "I need the real stuff," she moaned, "but if I drink it, the baby won't sleep."

"Maybe a couple of deep, cleansing breaths and a quick walk up and down the street would do the trick," said Lucy.

Molly looked at her as if she were speaking Chinese. "I don't think so," she said. "I can barely sit."

"Well, you don't even have to sit for your day at the spa," said Lucy. "You can recline in luxury."

"I honestly think I'm too tired to get there," said Molly, miserably. "I was up all night with the baby."

"He was fussy with us," admitted Lucy. "Did you try letting him cry it out?"

"We tried, but he wouldn't stop crying. I think it made things worse."

"He's quiet now," observed Lucy.

"That's the problem. He sleeps all day and cries all night."

"Sometimes it takes them a while to get sorted out," said Lucy.

"Why doesn't anybody ever tell you what it's really like? That you'll never get to sleep, that your clothes and hair smell like sour milk, that your stomach feels like bread dough?"

"That's simple," said Lucy, pulling Molly to her feet. "If people knew the truth, they'd never have babies, and Homo sapiens would become extinct."

"I suppose you think that's funny," muttered Molly as Toby came into the kitchen to say good-bye. "Are you sure you can manage?" she asked him.

"Don't worry. Go. Relax. Enjoy yourself," he assured her.

"Maybe I should change the appointment," said Molly. "I don't have to go today."

Toby looked to his mother for help.

"Come on, Molly," Lucy said, taking her hand and leading her to the door. "Toby knows all about babies. He used to take care of his little sisters. He'll be fine."

"That's right," said Toby. "Now, go, or you'll be late."

For a moment, when they were getting in the car, Lucy thought Molly might cry, but she managed to distract her by chattering on about the weather, the flowers, even her odd little conversation with Tommy. Soon they were pulling up in front of the spa, where a uniformed valet took the car and a doorman greeted them.

Inside, the air was perfumed, the carpet

was thick, and a wall of water set a soothing tone. They were soon whisked away and wrapped in cotton terry robes and given herb tea to drink in the luxuriously appointed lounge while they waited for their massage appointments.

All the while Lucy was enjoying her massage, she hoped that Molly was having the same experience. She felt all her tension, all her aches and pains melt away under the massage therapist's skilled hands. Then she was ushered back to the lounge, where a light buffet lunch of fruit and salad had been set out. Lucy was happy to see that Molly had already helped herself and was stretched out on a chaise, tucking into a plateful of food.

"What do you think so far?" asked Lucy.

"To tell the truth, I'm not thinking at all," said Molly, popping a strawberry into her mouth. "I'm so relaxed, I don't think I'm capable of thought."

The spa was apparently doing the trick, thought Lucy, settling herself on a comfy recliner and spearing a piece of melon. Molly was already sounding more cheerful.

After they'd eaten, the next step was a natural clay body wrap guaranteed to remove toxins and rejuvenate the skin, a relaxing soak in a tub dotted with fresh flowers, and a facial. When Lucy emerged after her manicure and pedicure, she felt loose limbed and radiant, and definitely free of toxins, though she was thinking some rather impure thoughts about what she'd like to do with Bill when she got home.

"How do you feel?" she asked Molly, who looked better than she'd looked in months, with rosy cheeks and a smile.

"I wish I could stay here forever," admitted Molly. "I wish I didn't have to go home."

Lucy bit her lip, hoping this wasn't a sign of trouble. "Toby will be so happy to see you looking so refreshed," she said.

As they waited for the valet to bring the car around, Lucy debated whether she should share her concern about postpartum depression with Molly. Should she tell her that Toby was worried about her and remind her that if things ever seemed to be too much for her, she could always call them, that they were just a short hop away on Red Top Road? Or was that overstepping her role as mother-in-law? She'd just about made up her mind to broach the subject when the car arrived, and there was the business of tipping the valet and getting seat belts fastened, and then Molly wanted to know all about Sara's prom dress.

Lucy was describing it as they followed

the winding road that ran through the resort, taking them past the pool and golf course and finally, just before the exit, the tennis courts, where she recognized Tina, playing with her husband, Lenny. They were an unlikely pair of athletes — Tina in a short white tennis skirt that revealed her substantial thighs and skinny little Lenny, with his signature mop of curly hair — but they were surprisingly good players. Tina had plenty of speed despite her size, and Lenny had a powerful backhand.

Lucy was pointing them out to Molly when she heard a sharp pop and instinctively reached for Molly, pushing her head down and accelerating toward the shelter provided by a stand of rhododendron bushes.

"What's that?" asked Molly as several more pops were heard.

"It sounded like gunshots," said Lucy, whose hands were trembling as she clutched the steering wheel. The pops had stopped, followed by a loud silence. Lucy was trying to dial 911 on her cell phone, intending to report the incident, when she heard someone calling "Help" from the tennis court. Without stopping to think, she was out of the car, still clutching the cell phone, dashing around the bushes and down the slope to the court, where she could see Tina lying on the bright green surface. Lenny was standing beside her in bloodstained clothes, shouting. Taking in the scene, Lucy stopped to check her phone. The call hadn't gone through, so she quickly punched in the numbers again. Molly caught up to her just as she was telling the dispatcher that there had been a double shooting at the Salt Aire tennis courts. When she finished, Molly tapped her shoulder and pointed. Together, they watched a figure dressed in white, with shiny blond hair, running through the woods on the other side of the tennis courts.

CHAPTER EIGHT

Molly immediately began galloping down the hill, weaving her way between trees and whipping through straggly bits of undergrowth, while Lucy followed, trying to keep up while she was talking with the dispatcher.

"A shooting at the Salt Aire tennis courts," she panted. "A woman down. I think it's Tina Nowak. Her husband may be hit, too."

"Is she breathing?"

Lenny, who had been cradling his wife in his arms, changed position slightly, and Lucy saw bright red blood spreading across Tina's white tennis shirt. His shirt was also bloody.

"I can't tell. I'm too far away. There's a lot of blood on both of them. He may be wounded, too. The shooter ran away, on the opposite side of the courts," added Lucy, reaching the fence and following it to the gate.

"Rescue and police units are on the way,"

said the dispatcher. "Can you update me on the victims' conditions?"

"I'm almost there," said Lucy. Molly was already on her knees beside the couple, trying to extricate Tina from Lenny's grip.

"No, no, no," he insisted, shaking his head and pulling Tina closer.

"I have CPR training," said Molly. "CPR. It could save her life, but you need to let go so I can start."

Lenny didn't seem to understand but continued to cradle his wife, looking at Molly with an expression of bewilderment and shock. Then, as Molly repeated herself, he gradually loosened his grip and gently laid his wife down on the bright green surface of the court. Molly immediately sprang into action, positioning Tina's head, making sure her airway was clear, and then breathing into her mouth. After completing the two breaths, she placed her hands on Tina's chest and pressed. When she applied pressure, however, a small geyser of blood spurted from what appeared to be a shot to the heart. Her eyes round with horror, she looked at Lucy.

"Just do the breathing," advised Lucy. She turned to Lenny. "Are you hurt?"

He shook his head, then dropped to his knees beside his wife and picked up her limp hand, pressing it to his face.

Lucy could hear the sirens approaching and willed the rescue squad to speed it up, to hurry. Tina's life was spilling out onto the tennis court. Blood was now filling her mouth, but Molly continued to try puffing breaths through her nose until an EMT pulled her away. Lucy immediately put her arms around the shaking young woman, who began crying with deep, heaving sobs. Like Lenny, her shirt was smeared with Tina's blood.

"I tried. I tried," she repeated, burying her head on Lucy's shoulder.

Lucy could only hold her and stroke her head while the EMTs quickly transferred Tina to a gurney and loaded her into the ambulance. Another member of the squad, a woman, took charge of Lenny and led him to the ambulance, too. In minutes, they were gone, and the police were cordoning off the court. Their radios sent up a constant squawk, and the lights on the squad cars flickered like strobes. It all seemed very unreal and disorienting; Lucy led Molly to a bench, and they sat down, holding hands. A young woman officer approached, carrying tissues and a foil blanket.

"Sometimes, no matter how hard you try, it's not enough," the officer said, enfolding

Molly in the glittering silver wrap and seating herself beside them on the bench.

"Is she dead?" asked Molly, dabbing her face with the tissues. Her eyes were red rimmed and swollen, her face splotchy.

"I'm not a doctor," said the officer, "but it doesn't look good." She paused. "If she does survive, it will be due to your quick action."

She pulled out an official-looking notepad with a black leather cover. "Can you tell me what happened?"

"We were leaving the spa, driving along the road," began Lucy, "when we heard shots."

"How many?"

Lucy looked at Molly. "Four or five?" she asked.

Molly nodded. "About that."

Lucy went on. "I was afraid someone was shooting at us, so I drove to those rhododendron bushes and stopped the car, and I called nine-one-one on my cell phone and got out of the car. . . ."

"Why did you get out of the car?" asked the officer. "Why didn't you just keep driving?"

"I don't know," admitted Lucy, amazed at her own recklessness. "You can't just ignore something like that."

"We heard him screaming for help," said Molly.

The officer nodded. "What then?"

"Well, we could see Tina lying on the tennis court, and Lenny was yelling for help," replied Lucy.

"Did he have a gun?"

"No," said Molly, sniffling and pointing to the wooded hill beyond the tennis courts. "We saw someone running away, up that way."

"Can you give a description?"

Molly shook her head. "I only got a glimpse."

"Male or female?"

"I'm not sure. Like I said, it was a blur, a white blur," replied Molly.

"The shooter was wearing white?"

Lucy nodded. "Short blond hair. I noticed that. It was very bright in the sunlight."

"Then I got to the woman and started CPR," Molly interjected.

"And I stayed on the phone with nine-one-one," said Lucy.

"I guess that's all for now. I just need some form of identification," said the officer.

"Up in the car," said Lucy.

"Names and addresses then."

"Can we leave?" asked Molly. "I have a

baby at home who's getting hungry."

In fact, the blanket had slipped, and Lucy noticed that Molly's breasts were leaking milk, forming dark circles on her already blood-smeared blouse.

"Sorry. Detective Horowitz wants to talk to you." The officer gave a sympathetic little half smile. "He'll be here soon."

Indeed, Lucy spotted a plain dark sedan pulling into the parking area, which she suspected belonged to the detective, and a few minutes later saw him enter the fenced area, where he was met by the officer who had just interviewed them. He listened attentively to her report, then took a few moments to study the geography of the site before approaching them.

"Another body, Mrs. Stone?" he asked, one eyebrow raised as he stood in front of them. As always, he was dressed in a rumpled gray suit, and his thinning hair was also gray. He looked tired, with deep creases on either side of his mouth.

"Just bad luck," muttered Lucy. "Would it be okay if Molly went home to her baby?" she asked. "It's long past feeding time."

He nodded and called for an officer to drive Molly home.

Lucy watched as they hurried across the court, then turned to Detective Horowitz, who had taken Molly's spot beside her on the bench.

"I understand from your preliminary interview that you saw the shooter, whom you described as a person of indeterminate sex wearing white, with blond hair. Is that correct?"

"We only had a glimpse," said Lucy.

"Don't second-guess yourself," he instructed. "Just try to think back to that moment and tell me what you saw."

Lucy closed her eyes. "I was in the car, driving, when we heard the shots. My first instinct was to flee. I put my foot down on the gas and speeded up until I reached the bushes by the driveway. But when the shots stopped, we could hear Lenny calling for help. We kind of peeked cautiously around the bushes at first, but then we saw Tina lying there."

"You knew it was Tina?"

"Yeah, I noticed them as we drove past. I even said something to Molly."

"What did you do when you saw her on the ground?"

"Molly started running toward her, and I was following, trying to talk to the nine-one-one operator and trying not to fall or run into a tree, and I saw, I saw something white that caught my eye. I tried to get a better look, but the person was moving very quickly, running, almost leaping up the hill, away from me. The figure kind of came and went, you know, disappearing and then reappearing as she, I don't exactly know why, but I think it was a woman, as she ran through the trees and the shadows." Lucy raised her hand and pointed. "See that clearing there? It was flooded with sunlight, and when she ran across, I could see she had blond hair."

"Long hair?"

"No. Short, but it caught the light, you see. It was very bright. Unnatural, really. Maybe a dye job, or a wig."

He nodded. "You know, of course, that this shooter had to be a very good marksman. At least one shot went straight to the victim's heart."

"Tina's dead?"

"I think that's a safe assumption."

Lucy was silent, thinking. All of this seemed to point to Bar, but would the woman really shoot her rival? Finally, she spoke. "We got a press release last week at the paper announcing that Barbara Hume was named the Maine Gun Woman of the Year."

"Interesting," he said. "What color is her hair?"

Lucy didn't like being a tattletale, but she figured she wasn't telling Horowitz anything that the whole town didn't know. "Blond."

"Does she know the victim?" asked Horowitz.

"Oh yes. This is a small town, and they both have daughters in the same class at school."

"Were they friends?"

"Not really." Lucy paused, remembering the scene she had witnessed at the Mother's Day brunch and debating whether or not to tell Horowitz.

"Everybody knows they detested each other," she said, speaking slowly, reluctantly. "I saw them fight in the IGA over the last issue of the *Boston Globe*. And at a brunch, I overheard Bar tell her husband that when she was target shooting, she never missed if she imagined Tina's face on the target."

"Thanks," he said, standing up. "You've been very helpful."

"I wouldn't make too much of it," she said, calling after him. "It almost seems too pat, too easy."

It really did, she thought. It had seemed as if the shooter wanted to be seen. Why else would she wear white? If she had worn black and covered her hair, she would have been able to melt, unseen, into the shady woods. It was all very puzzling, and Lucy wanted to get to the bottom of it. But first, she knew she ought to call Ted to let him know they had a breaking story on their hands.

"Great work, Lucy," he told her when she'd finished. "Now I'll take it from here."

Lucy was dumbfounded. "What? It's my story. I broke it."

"Yeah, but you have your hands full right now. . . ."

"Not that full . . ."

"No. It's best this way. I'll take this, and you stick with the prom."

Lucy couldn't believe it. "The prom?"

"Yup." Ted wasn't about to argue. "That's my final word. Now I gotta go."

Lucy snapped her cell phone shut and sat for a few minutes, watching as the white-suited crime-scene officers examined every inch of the tennis court's surface. Other officers were combing the woods, looking for the spot where the shooter had stood. She heard a shout and saw someone waving from a patch of rock that offered a clear view of the tennis courts below. Players, absorbed in their game, would never have noticed the predator perched high above them. The thought made Lucy shudder, and she stood up, eager to get away from the evil that seemed to sit like a low-lying cloud over the place. She could almost feel it, like a dank morning mist that gave you goose bumps, and she hurried toward the gate, where Horowitz was conferring with a couple of officers. They moved aside to let her pass, but he held up his hand, indicating he wanted a word with her. She had to fight the impulse to flee while she stood a polite distance away, waiting for him.

Finally, he turned and approached her. "There was something I forgot to mention," he said.

Lucy knew what was coming. "I know, I know. Mind my own business. Leave this investigation to the professionals. Well, don't worry. I'm not covering the shooting. Ted's assigned me to a different story."

"Well, good," said Horowitz, nodding. "If you don't mind, what's the other story?"

"The prom," said Lucy.

"The prom!" exclaimed Horowitz, chuckling. "You, covering the prom! That's a good one." He grinned mischievously. "I'll alert the rescue squad, tell them to keep an ambulance on standby."

"Ha-ha," said Lucy, who wasn't finding this the least bit funny. "Are you implying that I had something to do with this?"

"Well," he said, "you do seem to have a

knack for finding bodies."

"Pure coincidence. I was here for a relaxing day of pampering at the spa."

"You should demand a refund," advised Horowitz before turning and heading into the woods for the climb to the rocky patch.

For once she agreed with him, thought Lucy, walking along the driveway back to her car. This had hardly been the soothing experience she had been looking forward to. The blissful sense of relaxation she had felt after her massage was long gone; now it seemed as if every muscle in her body was clenched tight. Even worse, she felt exposed and vulnerable, as if she had a target painted on her back, and she had to resist the urge to keep looking over her shoulder. It wouldn't do any good, she realized as she dragged the car door open and collapsed behind the steering wheel, because if the shooter had her in her sights, she'd never be able to avoid the bullet.

CHAPTER NINE

Driving home, Lucy couldn't erase the image of that red stain spreading on Tina's white Ralph Lauren shirt, swallowing up the little embroidered polo player logo. Even at a gallop, he couldn't escape the flowing blood, and neither could Tina. This was no random shooting, not one of those frequent Boston drive-by shootings that hit innocent bystanders. Whoever had shot Tina had carefully chosen a spot that gave a clear line of fire and had deliberately and cold-bloodedly chosen her as a target.

But was Bar the shooter? She certainly had the means: she was recognized as a skilled shooter and owned guns. She also had had the opportunity, but for that matter, so had the whole world. Tina had been shot in plain sight. And what about motive? Sure, the two had been rivals, but that had been going on for a long time, and when Lucy interviewed them about the after-prom party, they had apparently agreed to disagree while working together on a shared project. She could hardly believe that they'd suddenly had a conflict strong enough to prompt one to kill the other. But, she admitted to herself, it could all have been a big show for her benefit. Her instincts weren't infallible. She'd been fooled before and likely would be fooled in the future. It was one of the hazards of reporting.

And she knew from her own recent experience with Sara that sometimes it was difficult for a mother to separate her emotions from those of her child. If Bar had felt that Ashley was somehow threatened by Heather, she might have come to the tortured conclusion that killing Tina, Heather's mother, would somehow tip the scale in Ashley's favor. But that, she decided, would mean that Bar was seriously unbalanced, and that did not seem to be the case at all.

Approaching the turn onto Red Top Road, Lucy sped up. She was eager to reach the safety and security of home, but as she tooled along the wooded road, she had a sudden mental replay of the shooter fleeing through a similar landscape. All she'd seen, really, was that blond head of hair and a blur of white shirt, and once again, she thought it was an odd outfit for an assassin to choose. It was almost as if the shooter had wanted to be seen and identified. But why? Was Bar hoping that the jury would buy the argument that she would never have behaved so stupidly, especially right after the Gun Woman of the Year Award was announced? Or, thought Lucy, turning into her driveway, had Bar been set up by someone else?

"Gee," observed Bill as she entered the kitchen, "I thought you'd come home glowing and relaxed. You look like you've just witnessed a train wreck."

"Kind of," said Lucy, slipping her arms around his waist and resting her head on his chest. "Tina Nowak got shot on the tennis court at the spa."

Bill jerked away. "What?"

"Molly and I had a lovely time, we both felt great, and we were on our way home, driving past the tennis courts, when we heard shots. She was down. Lenny was holding her. She was bleeding. . . ."

"Oh my God." Bill pulled her closer. "That's terrible."

"Molly tried to give her CPR, but the EMTs don't think she'll make it."

"Shot, right out in broad daylight?"

"Yeah. We even saw the shooter running away."

"Could you tell who it was?"

"I'm not sure, but it looked a lot like Bar Hume."

"Wow!" exclaimed Bill, shaking his head. "I mean, everybody knew they hated each other, but this is crazy."

"What's crazy?" asked Sara, coming into the kitchen and staring at her mother. "I thought a facial was supposed to make you look better."

"Your mother had a bit of a shock," said Bill.

Sara was opening the refrigerator door. "Like what?"

"Tina Nowak got shot on the tennis court," said Lucy.

"By Bar Hume," added Bill.

Sara dropped the bottle of tomato juice she was holding, and it began to flow onto the floor, oozing across the wide wooden planks.

Lucy stood watching as the red liquid pooled on the floor, just like Tina's blood had spread beneath her on the tennis court, and felt herself getting very dizzy.

"Whoa there," cried Bill as she slumped against him in a dead faint.

■ ■ ■ ■

Sunday morning was like Mother's Day all over again. Bill ordered Lucy to stay in bed while he made waffles for breakfast. Zoe delivered the tray, which had been decorated with a little bunch of pansies from the garden, and Bill followed with the morning paper.

"The shooting made the front page," he told her.

Lucy stared at the headline, which announced FATAL SHOOTING SHOCKS SMALL TOWN, then set the paper aside. It wasn't exactly a shock; she hadn't expected Tina to live, but she had hoped for a miracle. "I can't face reading that just now," she said, taking a sip of orange juice. Before she knew it, she'd polished off her entire breakfast of blueberry waffles with maple syrup, bacon, orange juice, and coffee.

She had set the tray aside and was perusing a glossy home and garden special section when the phone rang. It was Ted. "I guess you heard that Tina's dead," he began.

"I saw the headline," she admitted. "It wasn't really a surprise. Any new developments?"

"Police are still investigating," he said.

"No arrest?"

"Not yet. They're waiting for forensics."

"Oh," said Lucy. She could hear voices in Sara's room. Sassie and Renee had slept over the night before, and it sounded as if they were beginning to wake up.

"I'm shooting for . . . uh, sorry about that. I want to put out a special edition, so I need you to come in this afternoon. Is that okay?"

"Sure," said Lucy, somewhat surprised. Ted, always budget conscious, rarely ran a special edition. What was going on? Was he trying to impress a potential buyer?

"Good," said Ted. "You can write the obit."

Lucy was about to protest, but he'd already hung up.

She was studying a photo of a charming cottage garden that mixed flowers and vegetables in the home and garden special section when Sara passed her open door and did a double take. "Why are you still in bed?"

"Dad thought I should take it easy today because of the way I fainted yesterday," she explained. "He gave me breakfast in bed."

"Can I look at the paper?"

"Sure." Lucy passed over the front section, watching for Sara's reaction.

"Golly," she said, sitting down on the foot

135

of the bed. "Are they gonna arrest Mrs. Hume?"

"Ted says they're waiting to see if the bullet came from her gun."

"What's going on? Can we come in?" Renee and Sassie were clustered in the doorway, adorable with their sleep-mussed hair and pastel jammies.

Sara held up the paper. "Mrs. Nowak died."

"That's awful," said Sassie.

"Poor Heather," said Renee. "I can't imagine losing my mom."

The girls fell silent. Finally Sassie spoke. "We have to do something."

"Like what?" asked Sara.

"You know, what people do after somebody dies," Sassie continued, looking at Lucy. "What do people do?"

"Take the family food or flowers. Call and offer to help. Some people send cards, but I usually write a note. A note is nicer and more personal. . . ."

"We could text," said Sara.

"You could," agreed Lucy, reminded once again that she was hopelessly out of date, and that for this generation, text messages had replaced handwritten notes.

Sara pulled her cell phone from her bathrobe pocket. "What shall we say?"

"Do you always carry your cell phone?" asked Lucy.

All three looked at her. "Yeah," they said in unison.

"Oh," said Lucy.

"Oh, look. I've already got a text. It's from Emily. She says we shouldn't talk to Ashley, because her mom is a murderer."

The other girls were checking their phones. "I got one from Karen that says the same thing."

"Crystal wants to get Ashley in the bathroom and teach her a lesson," reported Renee.

"Hold on," said Lucy, stunned at this display of adolescent venom. "Number one, Ashley's mom hasn't even been arrested, and even if she is charged with the shooting, she's innocent until convicted by a jury, right? And two, even if she did lose her mind and kill Heather's mom, which we don't know, Ashley certainly had nothing to do with it. She isn't responsible for her mother. She's as much a victim as Heather is. Imagine what she's going through. How would you feel if your mother was suspected of shooting someone?"

"Well," said Zoe, indignantly, poking her head through the door, "I'd want my Mother's Day card back."

■ ■ ■ ■

Lucy wasn't too excited about having to work on Sunday afternoon, especially since it was another beautiful May day and, inspired by the newspaper, she wanted to work in the garden. The sprouting vegetables needed to be thinned, weeds were popping up, and she wanted to bed out some impatiens. The last thing she wanted to do was to relive the whole horrible scene, but when she passed Lenny's office and saw his ancient Volvo parked outside, she knew her duty and pulled into the parking space beside it.

Interviewing people who'd lost loved ones was the hardest part of her job, and the first few times she'd had to do it, she'd felt like a ghoul. She was shocked to discover, however, that oftentimes the survivors didn't see it that way at all. They generally appreciated having an opportunity to talk about the loved one they had lost and to let others know what a wonderful person the deceased was. Whether it was a soldier killed in Iraq, a teen killed in a highway accident, or an aged Alzheimer's patient who had wandered off and died of exposure, she almost always found people who appreciated their unique qualities and would miss them. She reminded herself of that as she knocked on the locked door.

Lenny answered himself, opening the door a few inches and peeking cautiously through the crack.

Lucy hoped Lenny wasn't going to be the exception that proved the rule, the survivor who couldn't bear to talk about his loss. "I'm so sorry," she began.

"Come on in," he said, opening the door wide to admit her. "I want you to know I really appreciate what you and your daughter did yesterday." He paused, blinking back tears. "Nobody could have saved her. That's what they told me."

"That was Molly, my daughter-in-law. We wish it had turned out differently."

"She didn't have a chance," said Lenny, shaking his head. He wore his hair long, in a big curly mop, which made him look a bit clownish, but today his grief was palpable.

"I'm supposed to write an obituary," said Lucy. "But if this isn't a good time . . ."

"No, it's fine. I just came in to check my calendar so my secretary can reschedule whatever I've got in the next couple of weeks." He sat down on one of the dated Swedish modern chairs that filled his waiting room, along with a colorful abstract rug and a number of thriving green plants, which she suspected were Tina's contribution to the decor.

Lucy sat, too, and pulled out her notebook. "Let's start with basics. Full name, parents, birthplace, stuff like that."

He sighed. "Florence Christina Kramer. Her parents, sadly, are still alive. Alice and Stanley. They still live in Forest Hills, in Queens. That's where she was born. She went to Pace University. That's where we met. She majored in political science. She loved politics. She worked on a number of campaigns, always for liberal Democrats. I guess that's no surprise."

Lucy smiled. "How did you two liberal Democrats end up in Maine?"

Lenny was picking up steam, carried along on a wave of comforting memories, finding that the past offered a soothing refuge from the painful present. "It was the eighties. The city wasn't a good place to live. I'd just graduated from NYU Law, and we decided to move to the country. We'd vacationed here a couple of times and really liked it. So I took the Maine bar exam as well as the New York, and when I passed Maine but failed New York — that's off the record, by the way — the decision was made for us."

"Was it a good move?"

"We never regretted it," said Lenny. "Though I have to admit, the irony of Tina leaving a crime-ridden city like New York and getting shot here, in quiet Tinker's Cove, isn't lost on me."

"Me, either," said Lucy. "It's a tragedy."

He nodded. "For me, and especially for Heather. She's absolutely devastated. I don't know what she's going to do without her mom. Tina was a terrific mother. I guess you know that. She was always involved. Class mother, president of the PTA. She started the Boosters Club at the high school to raise money for sports equipment and uniforms. She was working on this after-prom party to keep the kids safe. If she saw a need, she tried to fill it."

"Yes, she did," said Lucy. "Just last week I interviewed her and Bar about the after-prom party." She paused, weighing her next question, and finally decided to go for it. "Do you think Bar shot her?"

"I'm not going there," said Lenny. "The police are investigating, and I am confident they will find the perpetrator. I also have great faith in our legal system — it's the best in the world — and it's up to the court to decide guilt or innocence."

This sounded like a talking point; Lucy

wanted to get back to the personal. "What were her favorite things? What did Tina like to do?"

"Tina loved to travel, she loved to cook, and she loved to organize." He stopped and gave a rueful little smile. "She was an organizer, that's for sure. I know a lot of people found her pushy and overbearing. She was a New Yorker. That's the way she was. But she was always thinking of others. She had a heart of gold, believe me."

His voice was cracking, and Lucy felt it was time to wrap up the interview.

"Thank you so much for talking with me. Is there anything you'd like to add?"

Lenny's hands tightened on his knees, and he stared out the window, looking into the distance. "Only this," he said. "Tina didn't deserve this. She deserved to see her daughter graduate from college, get married, have kids. Tina deserved to be a grandmother. That's what was taken from her, and it's not right."

"No," said Lucy, reaching out and covering his hand with her own. "No, it's not."

As she left the office, Lucy was surprised to see Heather arrive in her shiny new Prius, holding her cell phone to her ear as she drove. She was so involved in her conversation, in fact, that she didn't notice Lucy, who had to jump out of the way to avoid being hit. Lucy wanted to express her condolences to the girl, and to warn her that even though she was undoubtedly upset, she needed to pay attention when she drove, so she stood by the rear of the car, waiting for her to get out.

The door opened and Heather jumped out, the phone still pressed to her ear, but when she saw Lucy, she lowered her head and clicked the phone shut. "Hi, Mrs. Stone," she said, her voice flat.

"I'm so sorry about your mom," said Lucy, wondering who Heather had been talking to. She knew all sorts of messages were flying around and hoped it had been someone supportive.

"I can't believe it," said Heather, pulling a tissue out of her jeans pocket and dabbing her eyes.

"We're all in shock," said Lucy, her heart going out to the poor child. It took all her willpower not to burst into tears herself. She couldn't begin to imagine what Heather must be going through. "I was just inter-viewing your father for the obituary," she said, speaking softly. "If there's anything you want to add . . ."

Heather shook her head. "Just say she was the best mom in the world."

Lucy blinked back tears as she scribbled down the quote. "I know how hard it is to lose someone you love. If there's anything I can do, please let me know. Just give me a call," she said, giving her card to Heather. "And by the way, be extra careful when you drive, okay?"

Heather raised her face and met Lucy's gaze with red-rimmed eyes. She sniffled and quivered. "Thank you so much," she said. Then she turned and, walking stiffly, as if the very act pained her, went into the office.

Lucy watched, thinking of her own girls and how anxious she was for them to grow into responsible, caring adults. What was going to happen to Heather without her mother to guide her? Who would help her with her prom dress? Who would tell her she'd look good in bangs? Nobody would ever love her as much as her mother had. Lucy was sure of that. Sure, mother-daughter relationships were complex and difficult, especially during the teen years, but as much as girls sometimes resented their mothers' interference in their lives, these resentments usually faded, and they came to appreciate their mothers. But for Heather and Tina, that rapprochement would never be possible, thought Lucy, reaching for her car door. It was just too sad.

CHAPTER TEN

"A loving wife and mother, Tina will be remembered for her zest for life," wrote Lucy. "Politics was her passion, and she was the longtime chairman of the Democratic town committee and enjoyed attending both state and national conventions. In 2004 she had the honor of nominating John Kerry to be the party's candidate for president at the Democratic State Convention. She was particularly devoted to protecting a woman's right to choose and was a board member of the NARAL Pro-Choice America. She was an enthusiastic sportswoman who enjoyed playing golf and tennis; she served several terms on both the town's recreation and golf committees. She was also a past president of the Tinker's Cove Parent Teacher Association and, until her death, cochair of the After-Prom Party Committee. She was a member of the American Association of University Women (AAUW),

Emily's List, and the National Organization for Women (NOW) and served on the editorial board of *Ms.* magazine."

Finally finishing the list of surviving relatives and noting that "in lieu of flowers, donations can be made to the Save Darfur Coalition," she sat back in her chair and sighed.

"Just writing about Tina makes me tired," she told Phyllis, who had come in to man the phones. The murder had already been picked up by the national media, and calls for information were coming in from everybody, from *Inside Edition* to *Tennis Magazine.*

"Well, I'm just happy I come from a regular family," said Phyllis.

Lucy considered Phyllis's cousin Elfrida, who'd gone through several husbands and produced six children before her thirty-fifth birthday, hardly regular, but she didn't say so. "Me, too," she said. "I don't understand what makes women like her tick."

"They're overachievers," said Phyllis in the same tone she might have used for sex perverts, drunk drivers, or animal abusers.

"The sad part was that she was pushing her daughter to be an overachiever, too," said Lucy. "It's fine to have high expectations, but you have to let your kids know that it's not a tragedy if they don't get the highest score on every test."

"These kids today are under so much pressure," agreed Phyllis. "Why Elfrida had to go talk to little Charlie's teacher because he doesn't know his multiplication tables is beyond me. He's only in fifth grade, for pete's sake!"

"Maybe she should get some flash cards. They worked great for my kids," said Lucy, who remembered drilling her children on their tables much earlier than fifth grade.

"Oh, right, like Elfrida has time to sit around holding up flash cards."

"Charlie could do them by himself. Just have him set the timer for five or ten minutes every day, maybe before his favorite TV show," suggested Lucy, sharing a tactic she had used with Toby. "No flash cards, no MTV, or whatever they watch now."

"Well, I told her that she'd be smarter to concentrate on teaching him his addition and subtraction. That comes up more in life, anyway."

"Good idea," said Lucy, somewhat dismayed about poor Charlie's future prospects. She was also wondering if she dared leave and go home, since she'd finished the obituary and really wanted to work in the garden, when Ted arrived, yanking the door open and setting the little bell to jangling as he bustled in.

"Bar's been arrested," he declared, tossing his Red Sox cap on the coatrack, followed by his jacket. "She's already in the county lockup, awaiting arraignment first thing tomorrow."

"That was fast," said Lucy.

"What? No bail?" asked Phyllis.

"No way. It's a capital crime, and the evidence is damning. Numerous eyewitnesses identified her, her Escalade was spotted leaving the scene of the crime, her gun matches the bullet that killed Tina, and her gloves have gunpowder residue. If there was ever an open-and-shut case, this is it. The DA is not giving an inch on this one."

"That's pretty ironic," said Lucy. "Bar worked hard to get him elected."

"As I recall, she insisted that Democrats are too soft on crime," observed Phyllis.

"Well, that came back to bite her, didn't it?" said Ted. "Look, Lucy, I want you to do a sidebar on moms who kill other moms, killer moms, whatever you can find."

Lucy thought of the little radish seedlings that were crowded together in their row, and the tiny, tender lettuce leaves that nobody but she would bother to pick for supper, and sighed. "Okay, boss."

She turned to Google and discovered

there were plenty of violent moms. There were moms who killed their own kids. There were moms who killed their husbands and boyfriends. There was a Texas mom who wanted her daughter to be a cheerleader so badly that she hired a hit man to create a vacancy on the squad. While lots of moms killed on purpose, there were also careless moms who killed by accident, like the two soccer moms whose SUVs collided, killing a toddler. There were even the killer mom chimpanzees of Senegal, who hunted other primates and ate them.

But by far the most common killer moms were the ones who killed their own kids, more than a thousand of them in the nineties alone. Psychiatrists who studied the phenomenon concluded that they tended to be young and inexperienced mothers, generally poor or experiencing financial difficulties, who had recently suffered a death or loss. They usually believed they were taking their kids to a better place, or at least getting them out of a bad place, and generally planned to kill themselves, too, although they didn't always follow through on that part of the plan.

Lucy found it all very interesting in a morbid way, but none of her research shed much light on Bar's case. She was not young and inexperienced, she didn't have any financial difficulties, and she was happily married to her cardiac surgeon husband. The only case that seemed at all similar was the Texas cheerleader murder, but Lucy felt it would be unfair to compare Tina's murder with that case before all the facts were in.

"Gee, Ted, I'm not really coming up with much," she said. "These killer moms generally take it out on their kids."

"Or their husbands," offered Phyllis. "Like that Bobbitt woman, who cut off his thingy."

"Good point," said Lucy. "All indications seem to confirm that Dr. Barton Hume's thingy is still intact."

Ted was not amused. "Very funny," he snarled. "What about that Texas cheerleader mom?"

"I have a problem with that one," admitted Lucy.

"What's the problem?" demanded Ted. "It's almost exactly the same. Pushy mother, in this case Bar, wants her kid to be valedictorian and kills to destroy the competition."

"If that's the case, why didn't she kill Heather?" asked Lucy.

Ted shrugged. "This way she gets rid of her own rival, Tina, and she probably figures that little Heather will be so upset about

151

her mother dying that she'll crack up."

"You're assuming a lot, Ted. What if Bar's innocent?" replied Lucy.

"Or maybe she killed Tina for another reason entirely," said Phyllis. "Like maybe because she was pro-choice and Bar is pro-life, or because Tina was a Democrat and she's a Republican, or because her husband is a doctor and Tina's husband is a malpractice attorney."

"That's brilliant!" exclaimed Ted, beaming at Phyllis.

Phyllis suddenly became very subdued. "What did I say? You've never called me brilliant before."

"Well, it's long overdue," insisted Ted. "Lucy, maybe you could stop by at the courthouse and see if Lenny Nowak has filed any suits against Dr. Hume."

"Sure," agreed Lucy. "I'll go tomorrow."

"Righto. Meanwhile, see what you can do with that sidebar."

"Okay, boss," muttered Lucy, grudgingly turning back to her keyboard. "You call the shots."

"Oh, I hope there's no more shooting," said Rachel, who had just come in and caught the tail end of the conversation. "We've had quite enough."

"There's never enough," declared Ted.

"Crime sells papers."

"You don't really mean that," said Rachel, looking shocked.

"Oh, yes, he does," said Lucy. "So what brings you to this dank and dark sweatshop on such a beautiful day?"

"Actually, I was hoping I could drag you away for a quick cup of coffee."

Lucy cocked her head in Ted's direction. "Ask Ted."

Rachel perched on the chair next to his desk and gave him a big smile. "You don't mind, do you? You're such a kind, generous boss. Lucy says so all the time."

Lucy and Phyllis watched with amusement.

"I'm sure you appreciate how a little break would help Lucy work even more brilliantly for you than she already does," Rachel added.

"I'm the brilliant one," said Phyllis. "How about taking me?"

"Sure," agreed Rachel. "How about it, Ted?"

"You can have Lucy for fifteen minutes — on condition that she brings back coffee for Phyllis and me."

"Why can't I go?" protested Phyllis as the phone started ringing again.

"Because I need you to answer the phone,

that's why." He turned to Lucy. "Cream and two sugars."

Phyllis sighed. "Black with no-cal sweetener for me."

"You got it," said Lucy, jumping up and grabbing her bag.

When they were outside on the sidewalk, Lucy tilted her head back to feel the sun on her face and took a deep breath, as if she could absorb the beautiful day and take it back inside with her. "So what's up?" she asked.

"Bar has asked Bob to defend her," said Rachel, referring to her lawyer husband.

"From what I hear, he's going to have a difficult time. Ted says the prosecutor thinks it's an open-and-shut case."

"I know that's how it looks," said Rachel as they walked along Main Street. The stores were mostly closed, and few people were around, except for a cluster of TV trucks around the police station. "But Bob says Bar insists she's innocent, that she was home taking a nap when the shooting occurred."

"Is there anyone who can confirm that?"

"Uh, no. She was alone. She didn't get any phone calls or anything."

"What about Ashley?"

"She was at Heather's house. They were

taking practice SAT tests."

"What a shame," said Lucy.

"I know. Bar could go to jail for life."

Lucy pulled open the door to Jake's Donut Shack. "That wasn't what I meant. I was thinking it was a shame for those two young things to be cooped up inside with SAT books on a gorgeous May weekend. Those girls ought to have been outside."

Stepping inside the coffee shop, Lucy and Rachel had their choice of tables. The place was nearly empty, except for a table full of out-of-town reporters. It seemed odd to Lucy, who usually went there in the morning, when every table was full, all the stools at the counter were occupied, and there was a line of people waiting for takeout. They decided to sit at the counter, as far away from the reporters as they could.

"Two coffees for here and two to go," Lucy told Jake.

"Don't usually see you in here on Sunday," he said, wiping his hands on a towel.

"Big story," said Lucy. "Ted's putting out a special edition."

"I thought I'd pick up more business," complained Jake. "Town's full of TV people."

"Give 'em time. They'll eventually find you," said Rachel.

"They're reporters, after all. They've all got inquiring minds," added Lucy.

"I'm afraid they've got closed minds," said Rachel. "Listen."

"I pity her lawyer, whatsisname, Bill Goodman," one beefy fellow in a CNN T-shirt was saying. "How's he gonna defend her?"

"Insanity?" offered a pert young blonde.

The group at the table laughed. "Never works," declared a guy with glasses, wearing a TruTV jacket. "Good thing this isn't Texas. There they'd already be getting the death chamber ready."

Rachel's face had gone very white, and Lucy wrapped an arm around her shoulder. "They're just gossiping," she said. "They don't know what they're talking about. They didn't even get Bob's name right."

"Fools," sputtered Jake, setting the mugs in front of them. "What do they know?"

"If only they were fools," said Rachel, lifting her mug and taking a sip. "The problem is that they're right. There's a whole lot of evidence against Bar. Bob's afraid they'll convict her in the media before she ever goes to trial."

"He could get a change of venue," suggested Lucy.

"Where? Antarctica? The Amazon?

China?"

"China's out. We already had a call from the New China News Agency."

"Well," said Rachel, "at least I can count on you and Ted to keep open minds and to remember that Bar is innocent until proven guilty."

"Well, you can count on me," said Lucy. "I'm not so sure about Ted. The police press conference made a strong impression on him. He said they were very confident they would get a conviction."

"Bob thinks Bar is telling the truth," said Rachel. "He's convinced that she's innocent, and that isn't usually the case. He's naturally pretty skeptical of most of his criminal clients, but not this time. He says his gut feeling is that she's been framed." She paused. "He wants me to tell you that he's put you on the visitor list in case you want to interview Bar."

"I might just do that," said Lucy, glancing at her watch and getting up. "I've gotta go." She picked up the bag Jake had ready for her and started digging in her purse for her wallet. "You know," she said thoughtfully. "Ted's been awfully bossy lately, more than usual. And Pam had a meeting or something last Thursday. Remember?"

Rachel's face was a mask. "So?"

"Well, Bob is Ted's lawyer. I wonder if he's mentioned anything to you? Like maybe about selling the paper, something like that?"

"Bob hasn't said anything to me," said Rachel, quickly picking up the check. "My treat."

"Trying to buy influence," laughed Lucy.

"If I could, I would," said Rachel.

"Take heart," said Lucy. "I was there. I saw the shooter. The police asked me for a description. And even as I was saying she looked like Bar, I felt that wasn't right." Lucy paused, thinking. "Well, that's exactly it, I think. She did look like Bar, but I didn't think it really was Bar, and I still don't."

Chapter Eleven

Back home, Lucy was still thinking about her talk with Rachel when she took a glass of wine into the family room and sat down for a little breather before making supper. She leaned back on a pillow, took a sip of chardonnay, and flipped on the TV to catch the evening news. What she saw made her sit bolt upright: A grainy black-and-white extreme close-up of Bar's face, with the words *Killer Mom,* filled the screen, accompanied by strident, attention-grabbing music. Thoroughly disgusted, she flipped through the channels, only to see the same theme repeated by all the networks that weren't showing baseball games or golf matches. Bar was described as a "murderous mom," "killer mom from hell," and "maniac mom." One station even went so far as to show a computer simulation of the shooting, complete with a blond-haired shooter resembling Bar running through the woods.

Even worse, details of the competitive rivalry between the two families were reported, and footage of Ashley and Heather, which looked as if it had come from the local station's sports department, was aired. They showed Heather skating in a recent competition and Ashley serving a tennis ball with a terrific thwack. Turning off the TV in disgust, Lucy wondered how many times the networks would replay that footage in the coming months, as the investigation continued and the case went to trial. Not that the trial mattered — it seemed that Bar had already been judged guilty and convicted of murder by the media. Even if Bob managed to pull off a miracle and she was found innocent, most people would believe she got off, and that the justice system had failed.

Sighing, she got up and went into the kitchen to start supper. Sunday supper was always a bit of a problem since the family tended to scatter on Sunday afternoons and she never knew when everybody would be home. Bill had recently taken up golf and spent most Sunday afternoons on the new town course. Sara usually spent Sunday afternoons at the Friends of Animals rehabilitation center, helping to care for sick or

160

injured animals, and May was an especially busy time, with lots of orphaned wild babies. Now that Zoe was older, she was enjoying more freedom to roam on her bicycle with her friends. Lucy usually kept it simple, opting for soup and sandwiches so everyone could help themselves, and tonight she'd planned clam chowder and tuna sandwiches. She had set the chowder on low heat and was mixing up the tuna salad, but her mind was elsewhere.

Sure, she muttered to herself, labeling Bar a killer mom sold newspapers, it caught TV viewers' attention, but it wasn't fair to Bar. She had as much right to a fair trial as anybody else, and as Rachel had said, it was going to be difficult to find jurors who hadn't already formed some opinion about her guilt or innocence. But as bad as this was for Bar, Lucy thought it was much worse for Heather and Ashley. They were trapped in this story like flies on sticky yellow flypaper; there was no way they could escape and go back to being regular, anonymous kids. She finished chopping up the celery and mixed it into the bowl with tuna and mayonnaise, then covered the bowl with wrap and set it in the refrigerator. That done, she wondered if there was any way she could turn this juggernaut of publicity in another direction. Write an editorial reminding everybody that Bar was innocent until proven guilty? Do a story on the negative effects of notoriety on teenage girls? Interview Bar and write the story from her point of view? Ted would never go for it, but even if he did, it would reach only a small audience of *Pennysaver* subscribers. No, she thought, the only way to change the dynamic would be to investigate the shooting herself and hopefully turn up some new evidence. She might, she admitted to herself, just find out that everybody was right and Bar was indeed guilty. But there was a chance that Bar was telling the truth when she claimed she was innocent. If that was true, it meant that a dangerous killer was still at large.

Ted wanted her to check out the courthouse for possible malpractice suits against Bart Hume; that would be a good place to start. And while she was at the county complex, she could also pay a visit to Bar in the county jail.

Lucy was stirring the chowder when Zoe came in. "Hi, Mom," she said. "Where is everybody?"

"Your father's playing golf, and Sara is at the shelter. She's going to be late, because somebody brought in five raccoon babies just as they were closing."

"I bet they're cute," said Zoe.

"I'm sure they are," said Lucy, remembering the spring they'd shared their attic with a rambunctious raccoon family. Those little masked faces had been adorable but very destructive and, being nocturnal, extremely noisy at night, when the thumps and bumps and snarls over their heads had sounded like a rugby match. It had been a great relief when they'd finally left and Bill was able to seal the attic so the mother couldn't return next year to raise another litter.

"Maybe she could bring one home for a pet."

"No way!" exclaimed Lucy, who remembered having to wear a face mask and rubber gloves to clean up the mess they'd left. Then, seeing Zoe's disappointed expression, she softened her voice. "Libby wouldn't like it very much, I'm afraid."

"You know, Mom," said Zoe, growing serious. "I've been worried about Sara."

Hearing this, Lucy's motherly radar switched to red alert. "Why have you been worried?" she asked, trying to sound casual.

"Well, when I was doing my homework yesterday, my pen ran out of ink, so I went in Sara's room to find another one. Her backpack was on her desk chair, and I opened it. I know I should have gotten her permission first, but I only needed to write a few words to finish my vocabulary sentences. Anyway, I found all sorts of medicine in there, but she's not sick, is she?"

"Not that I know of," said Lucy. "What kind of medicine?"

"Mostly diet pills and vitamins and some laxatives. There was something called Ipekicky or something like that."

"Ipecac?"

"That's it."

Lucy was stunned. She couldn't believe her beautiful, healthy, intelligent Sara was resorting to these extreme measures to lose weight.

"I learned in health class that those things are bad for you," added Zoe. "Using stuff like that can give you anorexia or bulimia, and those are bad news."

"Have you seen her taking them?" asked Lucy.

"No, but she's been real mean lately. Don't tell her I told, okay?"

"It's just between you and me. So, how about some supper?"

"Great. I'm starving," said Zoe.

Once Lucy ladled out some chowder and made a sandwich, she left Zoe to eat her supper and went upstairs. She hurried into

Sara's room and peeked into the backpack, but it was empty, except for a couple of notebooks. She had just finished searching the room, finding nothing, when Zoe called out that Bill was home.

When Sara came home around seven-thirty, Lucy sat down at the kitchen table with her and drank a cup of decaf. She said it was just to keep her company and chatted with her about her day, but she also wanted to make sure that Sara was eating, without alerting her to the fact that she'd been snooping in her room. She knew that would set off a firestorm. The food went down as Sara chatted about the baby raccoons, describing their antics. Lucy paid special attention to her movements that evening, and there was no sign she was spending a lot of time in the bathroom, but Lucy remained watchful.

When Lucy drove to work on Monday morning, she was shocked at the number of TV trucks parked on Main Street. A few reporters were even giving reports, looking rather silly standing on little step stools and flanked by umbrella-like light reflectors as they spoke earnestly into the cameras. A few were already in the *Pennysaver* office, demanding information from Phyllis, who was also trying to answer the phone, which was ringing constantly. "Where can you get coffee? Who's got the best takeout? What's the high school principal's name? What do you know about Bar Hume? Tina Nowak? What do you people do for fun?"

Arriving behind Lucy, Ted took charge. "This is Maine. We're New Englanders. We don't believe in fun," he declared, shooing them out. "I'd love to help you, but I've got a newspaper to put out," he said, shutting the door and flipping the sign to CLOSED.

"From now on we'll have to use the back door," he told Lucy as he shut the old-fashioned wood blinds on the plate-glass window. "Phyllis, for God's sake, switch the phone to voice mail. I can't hear myself think."

"Good morning to you, too," said Lucy.

"It's not a good morning," he replied. "I've got to get over to Gilead for the arraignment, the warrant for the town meeting just came in, all seventy-eight pages of it, and I can't go anywhere without having some network nitwit shoving a microphone in my face."

"It's a regular media circus," added Phyllis, adjusting her harlequin glasses.

"Well, it's a big story," said Lucy. "Where shall I start?"

"On the warrant, I guess," said Ted.

"The warrant? I thought you wanted me to do research over at the courthouse?"

"That's going to have to wait. Town meeting is next week," he said, speaking faster as he counted the issues off on his fingers. "We've got to print the warrant, and we've got to provide some budget analysis for the voters. They want a new police station for nine million dollars, for Pete's sake. Can the town really afford that? And what about the roof on the high school? That thing leaks like a sieve, but will voters go for an override that will raise their taxes? You've got to talk to the town manager, the selectmen, get their input. What's top priority? What can wait?"

Lucy couldn't believe what she was hearing. The biggest story to hit the town in years had fallen in their laps, and she was stuck writing about the town budget. "Okay," she said, hoping to negotiate a better deal. "Say I get this done lickety-split. How about I work on the lawsuit research this afternoon?"

"Sure, sure," said Ted, reaching for his Windbreaker and pulling the hood over his head and dashing for the back door. "I've got to get to Gilead."

"Be careful out there," advised Phyllis,

who was a big *Hill Street Blues* fan.

Lucy knew Ted was right. The shooting was a sensational attention grabber, but the town meeting's votes on the budget would impact taxpayers long after Tina and Bar were forgotten. She sat down at her desk, with a sigh, and flipped on the computer, where she found the town warrant waiting for her in her e-mail.

"Don't forget you have to format it," said Phyllis. "You can't copy and paste directly from e-mail. It comes out all weird."

"So it seems," said Lucy, watching the warrant dissolve into scattered words and phrases on her screen, which she would have to round up with her mouse. "I see a painful case of carpal tunnel syndrome in my future."

The peanut butter and jelly sandwich she'd had for lunch was just a memory when Lucy finally had the warrant in printable shape. She was just reaching for the phone to call the chairman of the board of selectmen when the police scanner began cackling and all units were ordered to the high school.

"Something's up," she told Phyllis at the same time she was making sure her camera and notebook were in her bag. "Hopefully, it won't take long, and I'll be right back."

"You go, girl," said Phyllis. "If you have to call, use my cell number."

"Got it."

Lucy felt like a member of the French underground as she stuck her head out the back door to check that the coast was clear, then remembered her car was parked on Main Street, right in front of the office. She hurried through the alleyway between the storefronts and dashed for her car, but she wasn't approached by anyone, and no microphones were shoved in her face. The reason became clear when she arrived at the high school, where trucks with satellite dishes lined the driveway and yellow tape had been strung around the building in an effort to keep reporters from harassing teachers and students.

Students who crossed the yellow line, however, were fair game, and a good number of students had decided to seek their fifteen minutes of fame when the dismissal bell rang, setting up a media feeding frenzy. The arrival of a squad car with blinking lights and blaring siren caught everyone's attention, and the chase was on as the pack took up pursuit, following it to the baseball field, where all the players and most of the viewers were engaged in a giant brawl.

Fists and elbows were flying; kids were

pushing and shoving; there were grunts, groans, and a great deal of swearing. The coaches and a handful of male teachers were attempting to restore order but weren't making much progress; Lucy saw Sara's science teacher take a knock in the chest before he grabbed two students by their collars and dragged them out of the fray. Tommy Stanton and Chad Mackenzie were in the middle, staggering around together like two boxers in the twelfth round. Some of the players had grabbed bats and were swinging them; one kid had the bright idea of throwing a trash barrel into the melee.

The sight stopped Lucy in her tracks. Recalling Sara's announcement at breakfast that she was planning to watch Chad play, she immediately began looking for her daughter and found her, along with Sassie and Renee and a few other cheerleaders, huddled beside the refreshment stand. Their faces were white with shock, and some, including Sara, were crying.

"Are you guys all right?" she asked, taking her daughter in her arms.

"Chad's in there!" exclaimed Sara. "He's gonna get killed!"

"The cops are here. It will be all right," said Lucy, fumbling in her bag and producing a rather dusty, crumpled tissue. "Here.

Wipe your eyes and tell me what happened. What's it all about?"

"Tommy started it," said Sara. "Tommy Stanton." Lucy wasn't sure whether this was the truth or if Sara was simply eager to pin the blame on somebody other than Chad.

"Is that true?" she asked the others.

"A guy on the Sharon team hit a high fly," said Sassie. "Tommy plays outfield, and he had it. He was right under it."

"But Chad — he's a second baseman — he ran back and got in his way, and they both missed the ball, and Tommy and Chad started fighting, and Sharon got four runs," said Renee.

"Then the guys on our team were yelling it wasn't fair, and then they all charged into the dugout to go after the Sharon guys, and then, well, you can see for yourself," said Sassie.

"Oh, my goodness," said Lucy, surveying the chaotic scene as three or four blue-uniformed Tinker's Cove police officers tried to subdue the battling mob. "Oh, I'm supposed to be covering this," she said, remembering her job and pulling out her camera to snap pictures. "You girls can wait for me in the car, okay?"

It was almost dinnertime when, thanks to reinforcements from the Sharon Police

171

Department, the last of the brawlers were captured and carried off in a school bus the police chief had commandeered for the purpose. Several kids were taken away by ambulance; others were taken home by parents who had heard about the fight and come to retrieve their children.

"What'll happen to the boys in the bus?" asked Sara when Lucy joined them in the car.

"I don't know for sure, but I assume they are under arrest and will be charged with creating a public disturbance or something like that," replied Lucy.

This was not what Sara wanted to hear. "Chad was in that bus," she exclaimed. "Will he go to jail?"

"They'll probably keep them in cells at the police station until their parents come to bail them out," said Lucy. She thought of the little row of three small cells in the basement of the police station. "It's going to be crowded, that's for sure."

Sara pressed her hand to her heart in a dramatic gesture. "I can't bear to think of Chad in jail!"

"I'm sure his parents will waste no time getting him out. The one you ought to worry about is Tommy. They took him away in an ambulance," said Lucy.

"I hope Tommy's okay," said Renee. "Chad had no business going after that ball —," she began but was silenced by a sharp look from Sara.

"You know she's right," said Sassie, defending Renee.

"I don't know any such thing, and neither do you," declared Sara, indignantly defending her boyfriend. "Since when are you the baseball experts?"

It was a tense drive home, and Lucy was relieved when she dropped off Sassie and Renee on Prudence Path and got Sara home. She put her to work making supper while she quickly wrote up an account of the brawl and e-mailed it to the *Pennysaver.* Then, when she was still sitting at the computer, her curiosity got the better of her, and she called up Sara's myspace.com account. Nothing much had changed, she noted, with relief. She didn't know what she'd expected — maybe a blog about losing weight or something like that. But the image of her daughter's smiling face remained unchanged, and she still loved animals and cheerleading. Only her list of best friends had changed. TS was gone, and CM had been added.

CHAPTER TWELVE

The clatter of pots coming from the kitchen seemed to indicate that Sara was occupied making supper, so Lucy decided she could risk a call to Molly, who as a twenty-something had become Lucy's adviser on the increasingly puzzling world of teens.

"I'm really worried about Sara," she began, keeping her voice low. "Zoe says she's got laxatives and diet pills. She's wild about this Mackenzie kid, but he's quite a bit older. There was a fight at the school today. I just feel as if the situation is spinning out of control, but I don't really know what's going on."

"Did you check her MySpace page?" asked Molly. Lucy could hear baby Patrick crying in the background.

"Yeah, but if there's a message there, I can't figure it out."

Molly sighed. "I think the baby's hungry again. I'll be right back."

Lucy waited, listening as Patrick's cries subsided to a whimper.

"I'm back," said Molly, sounding tired.

"He doesn't seem quite so cranky," ventured Lucy, trying to be positive.

"I checked the breast-feeding book, and it seems like he's having a growth spurt," said Molly. "I just have to keep nursing him until my supply catches up with his appetite. I feel like a cow."

"It'll catch up, never fear," advised Lucy. "And then he'll start sleeping more. Believe mc, I wish Sara was a baby again."

"I never looked at it that way," said Molly. "I guess I should be grateful he's still home every night. Like those bumper stickers. 'Do you know where your child is?' "

Lucy smiled to herself. It was good to hear Molly making jokes again. "So what about my baby?"

"Why not check her cell phone?"

"Sara would have a fit," Lucy said, considering the idea. "And besides, when would I get it? She's always got it with her."

"Just grab it sometime when she leaves it lying around. She'll think she mislaid it."

Now that she thought about it, Lucy realized that Sara was always wandering around the house, asking if anybody had seen her cell phone. It just might work. "I'll give it a try," said Lucy. "Thanks."

Next morning, Lucy was in the kitchen, pouring herself a cup of coffee, when she heard Sara banging around upstairs. Her voice came drifting down the stairs as she confronted Zoe. "What have you done with my French book?"

"What would I want with your French book?" Zoe replied.

"You know I've got a quiz. You want to see me fail."

"You're crazy," said Zoe, starting down the stairs.

"You know you hid it on me, you little weasel," snarled Sara.

The steps stopped. "I'm telling Mom," warned Zoe, resuming her descent.

Lucy took her coffee to the table and sat down, pushing aside a stack of books. Sara's books, she realized, with her cell phone on top. She quickly slipped it into the pocket of her robe and was casually sipping at her mug when Zoe exploded into the room.

"Did you hear her?" she demanded. "Sara says I took her French book."

"I think it's right here," said Lucy, pointing to the textbook.

Zoe went over to the stairway. "Mom found your stupid book!" she yelled.

Sara was down in what seemed like a single bound, grabbing her books and throwing her mother a wave. "You saved my life, Mom. Come on, Zo. I hear the bus!"

Zoe tossed her mother a look, rolling her eyes, and followed her older sister out the door.

Lucy remained at the table, sipping her coffee, expecting Sara to return any minute, looking for her phone. She heard the squeal of the bus's brakes, then the grind of gears as the bus started up again, and then the sound of the engine growing fainter and fainter. She got up and pushed the curtain on the door aside and looked out, checking that the driveway was empty. Then she hurried upstairs to get dressed and dashed over to Molly's house, using the path through the woods that practically led to her back door.

Molly was emptying her dishwasher when Lucy burst into her kitchen. "Shhh," she cautioned. "Patrick's napping."

Lucy nodded and showed her the phone. "I can't figure it out," she said. "It's all code or something. Like this one. P-nine-one-one. What does that mean?"

"It means 'a parent is watching,' " said Molly, taking the little flip phone. "It's a pain to punch in all the letters, so people who text a lot have developed a shorthand. P&C, for example, means 'private and confidential.' It's not too difficult once you get used to it." As she spoke, Molly was working her way through the messages. "Oh, lookee here. SSC. Somebody thinks Sara is super sexy cute."

"Chad maybe?"

"Probably. His initials are CM. And she's getting a lot of messages late at night, probably after you think she's asleep."

"That's what Elizabeth said."

"Yeah, like one and two a.m. This one calls her a fat ho."

"Maybe that's why she's got the laxatives."

"Maybe," said Molly. "Kids do talk that way, though. It could just be a reverse compliment. Like calling somebody 'bad' when you really mean that they're cool."

Lucy felt completely out of her depth here. "Who are the senders?"

"Well, there's a bunch of initials, but I'm not sure it means anything, because when these alpha girls start rumors, they often use other people's names in order to make it seem like everybody is in on it."

"Alpha girls?"

"You know, the queen bees, the girls who really work at being popular."

"They start rumors?"

"Some of these girls will do anything to stay at the top of the heap," said Molly, flicking through the list of calls. "When I was in high school, it was the two Jennifers. They drove one kid, Michelle Moore, right out of school. Her folks ended up sending her to a private school." She paused. "Look at this. Somebody called ASH is accusing Sara of offering to have sex with CM so he would ask her to the prom."

Lucy's jaw dropped. "No! Sara wouldn't do that."

Molly was quick to reassure her. "Of course not. It's a favorite trick to start a fake rumor. TS here says RUNTS, which means 'are you nuts?' and says he'll see her in school."

Lucy tapped her lip with her index finger, remembering the warning Tommy had given her about Chad. "Maybe that's what the fight was all about," she said. "Maybe Tommy Stanton thought Chad was going to take advantage of Sara."

"Could be," agreed Molly, who was still reading the messages. "Oh, here's somebody new, SK8TR. That must be skater. Ring any bells?"

"Heather Nowak is a figure skater."

"Well, she thinks Sara is lying to her,

DLTM, and warns her to QB, quit bitch-ing."

Lucy remembered the distraught teen she'd seen outside Lenny's office. "I can't believe that's really Heather, not right after her mother was shot."

"Pretty weird," agreed Molly. Soft cries were coming from Patrick's room, and she shut the phone. "My master calls," she wisecracked and hurried down the hall to his room. A few minutes later she emerged with the baby.

"Every time I see him, he looks as if he's grown," said Lucy, taking her grandson in her arms. "And he's sure getting heavy." But Patrick wasn't interested in being sociable; he wanted a second breakfast and dove for her breast. "Sorry. You need Mommy for that," she laughed, handing him back.

"Don't worry too much about Sara," said Molly, settling down in a rocking chair with the baby. "There were also some friendly messages from her GFs and BFFs."

Lucy ventured a guess. "Girlfriends?"

"And best friends forever. See? Even you can figure it out."

"Even a fossil like me."

Molly blushed. "You know what I mean."

"Thanks for helping," said Lucy, pulling the slider open. "I've got to get to work."

But first she had to go home and put Sara's phone someplace not too obvious where she'd find it easily. She finally decided to put it on the floor in Sara's room, sliding it under the unmade bed so it was mostly hidden by the drooping duvet. Then, giving the dog a parting pat on the head, she was out the door.

As she drove, her mind kept returning to the accusation Molly had uncovered. Lucy knew these things happened in high school; she remembered when Elizabeth was on the outs with her friends because she'd gone out for field hockey and they all wanted to play soccer. But that was all about Elizabeth making an unpopular choice, and when she stuck to her guns and refused to give in and switch teams, they'd eventually come around and let her sit at their lunch table again.

But this was different. These girls were attacking Sara's reputation, and that wasn't fair. Or was it? What if they were telling the truth? Mothers didn't know everything, she conceded to herself, but her intuition told her that Sara was flattered by Chad's attention but figured it probably wouldn't last. Was she right, or was Sara about to make a terrible mistake?

This was uncharted territory, and Lucy

had no idea what to do. If she confronted Sara, it would tip her off that her mother had been snooping into her private life, and she would surely be angry. And whatever influence Lucy had with her daughter would take a serious hit. Sara would assume her mother was in league with her enemies.

And if it was just a rumor, Lucy didn't see how Sara could fight it. The more she protested, the more legitimate the accusation would seem. And even more unnerving was the way this campaign was carried out in secret, away from adult eyes. When Elizabeth had had her difficulties, she'd received support from her teachers and coach, as well as her parents. But poor Sara was suffering alone, in secret. These messages were sent in a shorthand that most adults did not comprehend, and kids even had a special code to alert each other if an adult was present.

It was almost a relief when she arrived at the cemetery for Tina's burial and had to take off her mother cap and put on her reporter cap. For a little while, at least, she'd be too busy to fret about Sara. She joined the handful of cars parked in the cemetery, on the aptly named Lilac Drive, observing that the bushes were loaded with purple and white buds on the verge of blooming. Lilacs and cemeteries, they always seemed to go together, she thought as she got out of the car and made her way along the winding road to the grave site. Passing the parking area around the stone chapel, she noticed several TV trucks and felt a surge of sympathy for Lenny and Heather, who couldn't even bury poor Tina in privacy. Lenny had intended to keep the burial private, by invitation only, and to hold a memorial service at a later date, in hopes that by then the media would be busy elsewhere and Tina's life would be the subject of the service, rather than the sensational way in which she died. But somebody hadn't been able to resist the temptation to pass along a tip. The funeral director had ordered the reporters and cameramen to stand at a distance, however, and a couple of serious, young, black-suited assistants were making sure they obeyed.

The service was already under way when she joined the small group standing around the neat rectangular hole that had been cut in the ground. Tina's coffin was lying beside it, a simple pine box with only a small bunch of lily of the valley, obviously hand-picked, lying on top.

Lucy scanned the group, recognizing a few neighbors. An elderly couple, looking extremely frail and somber, must be her parents, she thought, feeling a surge of sympathy for them.

"Today we return the body of Florence Christina Nowak to the earth, from which she came," began the minister, Rev. Tom Sykes, from the nondenominational community church. "She was a friend, a sister, a wife, a mother. She believed the world could be a better place and worked hard to make it so. She was respected and admired, remembered not only for her good works but for the spirit of love and compassion and generosity that she brought to everything she did. May she rest in peace."

And then the coffin was lowered into the grave. Lenny stepped forward and tossed a handful of dirt on top, then stepped back. His face was expressionless, Lucy noticed. She was having a hard time herself, blinking back tears and trying not to sniffle in the quiet that had grown so very loud, but Lenny seemed to have his emotions well in check, and so did Heather, who stepped forward next and stooped down to pick up a handful of dirt. She tossed it on the coffin in an offhand, awkward motion and then stepped back to stand beside her father. The two stood there, a good yard apart, with stone faces, while the others filed past, some adding a handful of dirt, others simply bowing their heads.

The engine of the front-end loader that would cover the grave was already starting up when Lucy approached Tina's parents, Alice and Stanley, to offer her condolences.

"I'm so sorry for your loss," she said, taking Alice's palsied hand.

"Did you know Tina? Were you friends?" Alice asked eagerly. She had bright eyes, despite her age and the tremor in her hand; she looked like a wizened and shriveled version of Tina.

"We were working together on a committee to plan an after-prom party," said Lucy. "My name is Lucy Stone."

"Tina was a great one for committees," said the father, Stan. He was neatly dressed in a white shirt and charcoal gray suit, but his eyes drooped, so that the insides of his bottom eyelids showed, and he had to keep dabbing away his tears with a white cotton handkerchief.

"She will be missed," said Lucy, giving his hand a little squeeze. She was aware that others were waiting to speak to the old couple, so she moved on, looking for Heather and Lenny, but they were nowhere to be found.

CHAPTER THIRTEEN

Back at the office, Lucy was trying to write a moving description of Tina's bare-bones burial service, but Phyllis, who had already gotten several critical reviews from her friends, was expressing her disapproval.

"I never heard of a funeral without some sort of refreshments for the mourners," she said indignantly. "I mean, people give up their time to stand around a grave. The least you can do is give them a bite to eat."

"It was very brief," said Lucy, eyes fixed on her computer screen. "The whole thing didn't take more than fifteen minutes."

"And what was that all about?" demanded Phyllis. "Nobody had a nice word to say about the woman? She was on all those committees, she did all that work, and nobody wanted to recognize that?"

"This was just the burial," said Lucy. "There's going to be a memorial service later, when things have settled down."

"If you ask me, now's the time to have the service. People's nerves are all on edge. We could all use some closure."

"It would have been a media circus," said Lucy. "I don't blame him, really. He probably wants to remember his wife for herself, for her achievements, rather than as the victim of a sensational murder."

"Mark my words," predicted Phyllis. "There isn't going to be any memorial service. People always say there will be because they're too lazy or cheap to organize a decent memorial. I bet she never gets a tombstone, either."

Lenny had been very subdued, but he hadn't really shown any emotion at all, and Lucy wondered if Phyllis might be right. "I like to think Bill and the kids would shed a tear or two if I died tomorrow," she said.

"Don't tell me! He didn't even cry?" Phyllis was incredulous, her eyes practically popping through her black-and-white-striped reading glasses.

"Not a tear, not even a sniffle, from him or Heather, for that matter. But," Lucy quickly added, "a lot of people have trouble expressing emotion."

Phyllis shook her head. "That poor woman." She clucked her tongue. "We all cried at my mother's service. Even the garbageman was in tears. You'd think Tina's husband could work up a tear or two. And I hear Bar's husband is no better."

Lucy remembered Bart's composure at the Mother's Day brunch, when his wife was making a scene. "He does seem to be a bit of a cold fish, I'll give you that. I guess it goes with being a surgeon. You wouldn't want him getting all upset when he opened up your chest, now would you?"

"Cold fish?" sputtered Phyllis. "Not on your life."

Lucy was surprised. "What do you mean?"

"Well, like my dear departed mother used to say when she was still alive and before we gave her a big funeral, with a mahogany casket and four hired limousines and a catered reception with hot hors d'oeuvres, the word at the hospital is that Dr. Bart is hot to trot."

Lucy stopped typing. "Are you saying that Dr. Barton Hume, the eminent cardiac surgeon, church deacon, and deputy sheriff, is looking for romance outside the bounds of marriage?"

"Well, he asked Elfrida if she'd like to see his koi collection."

Bart? Koi? Elfrida? Lucy felt as if she'd entered an alternate universe. "How does he know Elfrida?"

"Ever since she got that job at the hospital. In billing."

"Elfrida's working in the billing department at the cottage hospital?" Lucy could only imagine the chaos that Phyllis's cousin would cause.

"Can you blame her? With six kids and another on the way, she's desperate to get out of the house. Plus, she needs the health insurance."

"So you're telling me Bart Hume hit on a pregnant woman?"

"She never shows much until the sixth month or so."

"Even so. He's married. She's married. . . ."

"Separated. And, of course, she does have a bit of a reputation for being, well . . ." Phyllis paused, searching for the right word.

Lucy supplied it. "Affectionate?"

"Exactly."

Lucy went back to her story, struck with the possibility that the reality of these two supermoms' lives was very different from the appearance of perfection they presented to the world. Until the shooting, she had taken them at face value as two accomplished, talented women who found themselves with time on their hands and turned to good works, as many women fortunate enough not to have to work for their supper have done for centuries. But now the rumor mill was running at top speed, grinding out speculations that Tina had not been the adored center of the Nowak household, and that Bart's attention wasn't focused on his jailed wife's plight. Were the gossips on to something, or was it just a lot of spite?

Lucy finished up the story, then sat for a moment, considering what to do next.

"When's Ted due back?" she asked.

"He's going to be at that global warming conference at the state university all day," said Phyllis. "He might even stay overnight, if he runs into some friends and they organize a dinner and he has a few drinks." Or maybe, thought Lucy, he'd be meeting with a possible buyer. It would be the perfect occasion if he was intending to cash in and sell the little independent weekly to a chain.

"I didn't realize that," said Lucy, deciding there was no sense worrying about something she had no control over. Instead, she considered the possibilities opening before her now that she was free to choose her next assignment. "Have you got the listings under control?" she asked.

"Pretty much," said Phyllis. "Why? Are you thinking of leaving early?"

"Not exactly," said Lucy, reaching for her bag and checking that her camera and notebook were inside. "I've got an interview."

"Who with?" asked Phyllis.

"The Gun Woman of the Year."

But first, before she tackled Bar, Lucy wanted to follow up on Ted's suggestion that she check the court records for possible malpractice suits against Dr. Bart. The county jail was an imposing presence, rather like a grim medieval castle, that stood on a hill overlooking the parking lot and the other buildings in the county complex: the courts, the district attorney's office, and the agricultural extension building. Her business was in the clerk's office at the superior court, where she went straight to one of two computers that contained lists of all the pending civil suits.

She clicked on the SEARCH icon and typed in "Dr. Barton Hume," but came up empty. She also typed in Bar's name, but there was no match. Lenny's name came up in a few class action suits, but they had to do with pollution by oil and paper companies. He was also representing the National Fund for Endangered Wildlife in an effort to block a real estate development company. But she couldn't find anything that involved either of the Humes.

Leaving the stately courthouse, Lucy started the long climb up to the jail, which was surrounded by miles of chain-link fence topped with vicious-looking razor wire. Lucy hated going there. She even hated looking at the building, which was so obviously a prison, but the worst part was actually going inside and hearing that solid metal door clank shut behind you. It made even a brief visit feel like a life sentence. But the women's wing, to give the correction authorities some credit, was slightly less grim than the men's. For one thing, it was located in a newer, more modern section built in 1960s cinder-block bland. The windows weren't barred, although Lucy suspected they were made of extra-thick glass, and the women were housed in dormlike rooms rather than barred cells. There were no luxuries, to be sure, but the place was clean and didn't smell.

Bar, however, was not pleased with her accommodations or her companions. "Watch out for that one. The least little thing sets her off," she whispered to Lucy, indicating a very large, pasty-faced woman with short red hair, who was the only other inmate in the common room, which also served as a visiting room.

"Who you looking at?" demanded the woman, giving Bar a hard stare with eyes that reminded Lucy of little round rabbit poops. "You talkin' about me?" Like Bar, she was dressed in loose blue pants and a white Tshirt.

Her presence made Lucy uncomfortable; she'd hoped to speak to Bar alone. She wasn't quite sure what to do but figured a friendly gesture couldn't hurt and extended a hand. "Hi! I'm Lucy. What's your name?"

"Why you want to know?" demanded the woman.

"Just being friendly," said Lucy, continuing to smile. She was no psychiatrist, but it seemed pretty obvious to her that the woman had some mental problems.

The red-haired woman hesitated, apparently weighing the pros and cons of revealing this information before deciding to give it up. "It's Ann," she muttered. "Ann Flood."

"Ann is such a pretty name," said Lucy. "You don't hear it much anymore."

"It's kinda plain," admitted the woman. "I named my daughters Amethyst and Sapphire."

It was clear to Lucy that this homely, confused woman had given her daughters fancy names because she hoped their lives would be better than hers, and she was deeply touched. "They're your family jewels," she said. "How old are they?"

"Eight and five," mumbled Ann, dropping her aggressive attitude. "I don't get to see 'em too much. They live with my mom now, over in Bridgton."

"I'm sure they miss you," said Lucy. "My friend, here, Bar, has a daughter, too." When Bar remained silent, Lucy prompted her. "How old is Ashley now?"

"Almost seventeen," said Bar, reluctant to be drawn into the conversation.

"Has she come to visit?" asked Ann.

"No," admitted Bar. "Her father and I decided it was better if she didn't come."

"Yeah, prob'ly for the best," agreed Ann. "Well, I'll let you two get on with your visit."

"Thanks," said Lucy, watching as she shuffled out of the common room.

"You see the sort of people I have to put up with," complained Bar, rolling her eyes. "That woman spat at a guard the other day."

"Everybody has bad days," said Lucy, checking to make sure she was really gone.

"Is this a friendly visit, or are you here to interview me?" asked Bar in a challenging tone. They were seated at a round table with fixed stools, like the ones in fastfood restaurants, only this one was scratched and gouged.

"A little of both," said Lucy. "I came on my own, at Bob Goodman's request. I don't have to write a story, if you don't want."

"Oh, I want," declared Bar. "I want everyone to know how badly I'm being treated, how unfair this is, how I'm absolutely one hundred percent innocent!"

"Got it," said Lucy, opening her notebook, along with a ballpoint pen, the only things she was allowed to bring in with her. "You know the prosecutor thinks this is an open-and-shut case, don't you?"

"I was framed!" exclaimed Bar. "Isn't it obvious? I'm not a criminal. I'm a law-abiding citizen. I shouldn't be here."

"The judge thought differently," said Lucy. "He denied bail."

"Can you believe it? You work all your life to make things better, to be a good person, and this is what you get! When I think of all the money I raised for the hospital and the library and the schools, well, it really makes me mad. All for nothing. Nobody took the time to look at the whole picture, to ask what kind of person I am. They just put gun woman and dead person together and locked me up. Even that rat of a prosecutor. I campaigned for him!"

"There were eyewitnesses who identified you."

"A blond woman! It could've been any one of millions of women. I'm not the only blonde in town. And anybody could buy a wig, couldn't they?"

Lucy nodded, writing it all down. "But you had a long-standing feud going with Tina. Everybody knew that."

"Friendly competition, that's all it was! Isn't this America? Isn't competition supposed to be a good thing? Don't we encourage our kids to compete? Isn't competition the name of the game?"

"Sometimes it goes too far," suggested Lucy.

Bar rolled her eyes. "Look, calling it competition was really an exaggeration, don't you agree? I mean, let's face it, Tina was a lovely woman — you won't find me speaking ill of the dead — but she really couldn't hold a candle to me, now could she? She was married to a sleazy lawyer. I'm married to an eminent surgeon. Her daughter is smart, but not exactly Mensa material, if you know what I mean. My house is on the National Register of Historic Places. Hers has a grass roof! My house is filled with Sheraton and Hepplewhite antiques. Her furniture comes from IKEA. I went to Rosemary Hall and Vassar. She went to public high school and some college I never heard of." She gave Lucy a condescending smile. "I could go on and on, but my point is that I had no reason to be jealous of Tina, and I had no reason at all to kill her."

"Okay," agreed Lucy. "Who did?"

"Lots of people! She was crude. She could be very insulting if you disagreed with her."

"Right," said Lucy. "But murder?"

"She was quite outspoken about keeping abortion legal," said Bar, pursing her lips.

"You think she was on one of those pro-life radicals' hit lists?"

"Search me. I don't have any contact with those people, but she very well could have been."

Lucy made a note to follow up on Bar's suggestion.

"And then there's the fact that her husband is a personal injury lawyer — an ambulance chaser. He must have made a lot of enemies through the years."

Lucy's research at the courthouse indicated this wasn't true, but she decided not to contradict Bar, in hopes of getting more information. "How so? Doesn't he help people who were wrongfully injured get some compensation?"

Bar scoffed at that idea. "You've seen too many TV commercials." She looked straight in Lucy's eyes. "Have you ever been sued?"

"Actually, no."

"Well, let me tell you, it's a horrible experience. You're bombarded with paperwork, you have to answer questionnaires and give depositions under oath, you have to hire a lawyer to represent you at great expense, while the person who's suing you pays his lawyer only if he wins, and you can't sleep, worrying that you're going to lose everything you've worked so hard for. It's a complete and utter nightmare. And even if you win the case and the jury agrees that you've done nothing wrong, you're stuck with enormous legal bills."

"I hadn't realized," said Lucy. "Have you actually gone through that yourself?"

"No, thank goodness. But even so, you wouldn't believe what Bart has to pay for malpractice insurance. It's thievery. And all because of those personal injury lawyers, out to make a buck. They're like turkey vultures, always looking for something nasty." Bar's expression brightened. "Maybe Lenny was the target, and the shooter missed."

"The police seem to think the shooter was an expert shot. Tina took at least one round right in the heart."

Bar's expression brightened. "That must be it! A jealous woman."

"Lenny and Tina seemed to be quite devoted," said Lucy, remembering the couple on the tennis court.

"*Seemed* is exactly right," crowed Bar. "It's no secret Lenny will chase anything in skirts. He's not like my Bart, who's faithful to his core. I simply can't imagine my Bart taking an interest in anyone but me. He's often said to me that you don't go looking for rhinestones when you've got the genuine thing."

Lucy swallowed hard, remembering what Phyllis had told her. "Even the most stalwart husband can have a wandering eye," she suggested.

"Oh, not Bart," scoffed Bar. "He's a devout churchgoer, a deacon. He knows adultery is a sin, and he'd never risk his immortal soul for some floozy."

Lucy pictured Elfrida, with her scoop-necked tops that revealed plenty of cleavage; and her short, short skirts that emphasized her long, long legs; and the way she kind of swayed her hips when she walked; and her easy, inviting smile. "I guess you never heard any of those blues songs about girls who make it easy for a man to do wrong."

"I don't know why you're going on about this," sniped Bar. "My husband does not listen to the blues."

"Country and western?" It was out before Lucy could catch it.

Bar narrowed her eyes. "Are you thinking of someone in particular?" she demanded.

Actually, Lucy was thinking of Elfrida's favorite hangout, the Rainbow Inn and Motel out on Route 1, but she didn't think she'd better mention it.

"Just rumors," she said.

"Well, doesn't that just take the cake!" exploded Bar. "It's not bad enough that this town has accused me of murder and has got me locked up like a rat in a cage, but now they're spreading malicious rumors about my Bart!"

"Maybe you should sue someone," quipped Lucy, immediately regretting her words.

"Get out!" screamed Bar. "Get out of here before I . . . I . . . I . . ."

"I didn't mean that," said Lucy, apologizing, but Bar was having none of it. Her face was red with fury.

"Guard! Guard!" shrieked Bar. "Take her away!"

"I'm going. I'm going," said Lucy when two uniformed officers appeared in the doorway. "No problem."

In the hallway she passed Ann. "That is one freaky lady," said Ann.

Takes one to know one, thought Lucy, amused. "She better not do that in front of a jury."

"You said it," agreed Ann. "If she pulls a fit like that, she'll be here for life."

CHAPTER FOURTEEN

April showers were supposed to bring May flowers, but thanks to global warming or climate change or maybe just never predictable New England weather, spring's advance was put on hold as chilly temperatures, gray skies, and showers stalled over the region. Lucy found it difficult to maintain her usual cheerful outlook on life, and she suspected it wasn't just the weather. Sara was secretive and hostile at home, and work wasn't much better, with Ted's bossy attitude and relentless focus on productivity. Instead of the two or three stories Lucy was used to writing, he now wanted four or five, and Lucy felt the pressure. It made for a lot of tension in the formerly relaxed office.

Lucy found herself looking forward to her Thursday morning breakfast with the girls as an opportunity to blow off some steam and get some positive support, and maybe even some helpful ideas for coping with

Sara. But she soon discovered that the girls were just as fixated as everyone else in town on the shooting.

"Doesn't it bother you that these two women who worked so hard to achieve perfection have come to such tragic ends?" she asked. "It all seems so sad to me."

"Not to me," said Sue, thoughtfully tapping her pointed little chin with a scarlet-tipped finger. "What happened to Corinne Appleton, that's a genuine tragedy, and I can't imagine what her poor parents are suffering. But Bar and Tina! You reap what you sow, and they weren't really nice. They were always putting others down in order to make themselves seem better."

"It's like what happened to Martha Stewart," said Pam, nodding her head and making her dangling silver earrings bounce. "A lot of people were happy to see her taken down a peg when she went to jail."

"I think people find it a relief when these people they thought were so perfect turn out to be no better than anybody else," said Rachel, fingering the reading glasses she wore on a chain around her neck. "Like suddenly it's okay to be average."

"Maybe it's even better to be average," said Sue.

"Exactly," agreed Rachel. "Good enough

is just fine."

"Okay, I understand that," admitted Lucy. "But do people have to dissect every aspect of their lives? What about those poor girls? They've not only lost their mothers but everybody's talking about their fathers, too."

"I'm surprised at you, Lucy," said Pam. "You're usually so keen on exposing the truth."

"I feel sorry for Lenny and Bart, too, if you want to know the truth," said Rachel. "Their wives were so driven and self-centered, when all men really want is a little attention. And now, one's a widower and the other's wife is in jail. They've actually both lost their wives."

"You know what would be really funny?" asked Sue, setting down her coffee cup, with a sly smile. "What if the two husbands conspired? After all, they've both managed to get rid of their wives now that Tina's dead and Bar's in jail."

"Well, if that's the case, they've seriously miscalculated," said Lucy, mopping up the last of her egg with the second piece of buttery toast — the one she had vowed not to eat.

"How so?" asked Pam.

Lucy popped the toast in her mouth. "Because now they're each saddled with a teenage daughter. And those girls make Paris Hilton look like a Girl Scout."

"Now you're the one who's spreading slander," said Rachel, raising an arched eyebrow. "From everything I've seen, they're attractive, talented, hardworking, high-achieving young ladies with bright futures. And now they're both missing their moms. It must be awful for them."

"That may be," admitted Lucy. "But their own troubles haven't stopped them from making Sara's life a living hell, spreading vile rumors about her with their cell phones and computers."

"Oh, honey," said Sue, reaching out and patting her hand. "I know you're feeling like a mother bear ready to defend her cub, but it's not as bad as you think. It's the same old, same old. I remember when Sidra was in high school, and somebody started a rumor that she was pregnant when she actually had mono and had to stay out of school for a couple of months."

"That's right," chimed in Pam in a rather superior tone. "That's why I was so glad to have Tim. Girls are nasty and devious and always have been. It just seems worse now because of text messages and myspace .com."

"No, it is worse," insisted Lucy. "When

we were in high school, the girls could make fun of your underwear when you changed for gym or tease you about your little boobs or your big butt, but now they have cell phone cameras, and they can take your picture and send it to the entire football team, including your boyfriend."

"So what? Sara's got a lovely figure," said Pam, complacently. "I seem to remember she was running around town in a rather racy little bikini last summer."

"But this is different," insisted Lucy, who didn't like being reminded yet again of the bikini episode. "She was in control when she went out in the bikini, and to tell the truth, I don't think she had any idea that she was attracting so much attention. And I made her stop as soon as I heard about it. But this is something she has no control over. That's what's scary about it. Plus, you wouldn't believe the mean stuff they've been saying about her. They're claiming that the only reason Chad asked her to the prom is because she promised to have sex with him!" Lucy hadn't really intended to share this bit of information, but she hoped it would elicit an outpouring of love and support from her friends. She was soon to be disappointed.

"I know it's upsetting, Lucy," said Rachel,

"but Pam is right. It's the same stuff that's been going on forever. It's just the way the message is delivered that's different. The expert opinion seems to be that unpleasant as this sort of thing is for the victim, it seems to be a necessary phase of human development that helps teens emerge as caring and compassionate adults."

"I'm not convinced," said Lucy, put out at her friends' lack of outrage. "Maybe instead of turning a blind eye to this electronic bullying, we need to say it's unacceptable, like underage drinking. Everybody used to just shrug their shoulders at that until Mothers Against Drunk Driving came along and worked hard to change attitudes. Maybe we need to teach tolerance and acceptance if we want our kids to be tolerant and accepting."

"That's the other school of thought," said Rachel. "But I can't say I'm surprised at this behavior. Just look at their mothers! They used those girls as pawns in their silly little feud. They put so much pressure on them to outdo each other that they're bound to have inferiority complexes. They can't possibly live up to their mothers' expectations."

"I don't buy it," said Lucy. "Heather's made quite a name for herself as a figure skater. She must have a certain amount of confidence to get out there and compete like that."

"Maybe," admitted Rachel. "But you can be sure that unless she'd won the Olympic gold medal, her mother wouldn't have been satisfied."

"And now she's not off the hook," said Pam. "She probably feels like she has to dedicate every performance to her mom. I've seen it happen. The dead mother's influence gets stronger, like she's reaching out from the grave."

Lucy couldn't agree. "The way she's behaving toward Sara, I wouldn't be surprised if Heather pulled a stunt like Tonya Harding and disabled the competition!"

This got a few chuckles, but Lucy hadn't meant it as a joke.

"It's Ashley who worries me," said Sue, frowning. "She volunteered at Little Prodigies last term, and I never saw such a perfectionist. She must have been putting in hours and hours of preparation. If she read a story, she'd make little felt finger puppets of the characters to give to the kids. If they were finger painting, she'd mop up every drop and spatter the minute it happened. She was driving everyone crazy, including the kids. The teachers couldn't wait for tennis season to start. She's team captain, but you know what she told me? She said it's not a big deal, because hardly anybody plays tennis."

"There are only about six kids on the team," said Lucy.

"But she won the state championship last year," said Sue. "She must be very good."

"You know what I think is so weird about those girls?" asked Pam. "It's the way they look so much alike. They're both rail thin. They have those big eyes and identical hairdos. They could be twins. I see them together a lot."

"Well," said Rachel. "They have a lot in common. But maybe now that their moms are out of the picture, they'll eventually be freer to be themselves."

"Don't bet on it," said Sue. "Not for Ashley, anyway. Dr. Bart was all over her when she was working at the preschool. He'd grill her about everything when he came to pick her up. Was she on time? What activities did she offer the kids? Were they successful? On and on it went. It was weird." She paused, reflecting. "Very controlling. Dominating. I found it disturbing. Creepy, even."

"It's hard to believe he could be more controlling than Bar," said Pam.

"I know," said Sue, putting her hand to

her mouth. "And maybe I'm making too much of this, but you know, there was almost something sexual about it."

The women exchanged uncomfortable glances.

"That's really upsetting, if it's true," said Rachel.

Sue's cheeks colored beneath her carefully applied foundation and blush, and she shook her head. "Don't pay attention to me," she said, with a rueful grin. "I probably have an overactive imagination."

Once outside, Lucy took a deep breath of the cool, rain-fresh air and raised her umbrella for the short walk to the office. She usually left the Thursday morning breakfast with a smile on her face, but today it felt like a big cloud of sadness had enveloped her, like those voluminous black chadors that Muslim women had to wear. She was lost in her thoughts, walking slowly past the bank, when she encountered Lenny, who was wearing a tan raincoat and toting an overstuffed briefcase. He was small, she realized, barely an inch taller than she was and probably weighing about the same. His mop of curly hair was the biggest thing about him, but today even it seemed smaller.

"A closing," he said, seemingly embarrassed about being back at work so soon after his wife's burial. "It wouldn't have been fair to my clients to reschedule."

"Of course not," said Lucy. "Life goes on."

"People are so quick to judge," he said. "I really appreciate the sensitive way you wrote about Tina's" — his voice caught as he got out the final word — "burial."

"Just doing my job," said Lucy, glossing over the fact that she had struggled to write a nonjudgmental account. "I know this must be a hard time for you and Heather. How's she doing?"

"Better than I expected," said Lenny. "Of course, kids don't really understand that death is final, do they?"

"Don't ask me," said Lucy, with a shrug. "I only have four kids, and I'm just beginning to figure out what goes on in their heads."

"You're way ahead of me then," said Lenny, resuming the walk to his car.

"You know," began Lucy, following him, "there is something I think you should know."

Lenny turned to face her. "About Heather?"

"Yes," said Lucy, not at all sure she should continue. "I don't know. Maybe this isn't a good idea."

"Well, now that you've begun, you'd better tell me, don't you think?" Lenny sighed. "Otherwise, I'll worry all day."

"Okay." Lucy took a deep breath. "I don't want to make a big deal about this, after all, I know that Heather is going through a lot right now, but it seems she's been behaving rather badly to my daughter."

Lenny furrowed his brows and leaned forward. "In what way?"

"Oh, the usual. Text messages with untrue rumors, embarrassing photos, postings on MySpace, things like that."

"Sounds pretty typical to me," said Lenny.

Suddenly Lucy felt exactly like that mother bear Sue had compared her to. She felt herself growing larger as she filled with rage, and it seemed to her, she was towering over teeny little Lenny, ready to swipe him with an enormous clawed paw. She was actually beginning to raise her hand when she caught herself. "I've had just about enough of these lame excuses," she snapped. "Maybe mean girls grow up to be mean women, like two people I could name. And neither one has come to a good end."

Lenny's eyes blazed as he struggled to keep his emotions under control. "Okay, so maybe you had your differences with Tina, but she tried her best to be a good mother.

Maybe she wasn't perfect, maybe she stepped on a few toes, maybe she was misunderstood, and maybe a lot of people simply didn't agree with the positions she took on controversial issues, like a woman's right to choose and school prayer . . ." he said, beginning to sound a bit as if he were summing up for a jury. "But I know one thing, and that is that Tina did not deserve to die. She did not deserve to be shot down in cold blood."

"And my daughter may not be perfect, either," sputtered Lucy, "but she doesn't deserve to be tormented by your daughter."

"That's rather a strong word, isn't it?" said Lenny, attempting to walk past Lucy to his car, a beat-up old Volvo, which was parked at the curb.

"No. No," said Lucy, stepping in front of him and blocking his path. "If you heard your daughter crying night after night, you wouldn't think it was too strong a word."

"How do you know I don't hear my daughter crying, too?" demanded Lenny.

For a moment Lucy was stunned. Was it true? Was Heather sobbing for her mother? Were the hate messages a way for her to distract herself from overwhelming grief? "Is that true?" she asked, her voice almost a whisper. "Is she crying for her mother?"

Lenny dropped his briefcase and shook his head. "Actually, no," he finally said. "She hasn't shed a tear, and it worries me." Standing there on the sidewalk, with his sloping shoulders and slumped back, Lenny seemed like a defeated man.

"Everyone grieves in their own way," she told him. "There's no correct way."

"I know that," agreed Lenny, "but it doesn't seem to me that she's grieving at all, and it worries me." He paused. "There's something very hard about Heather. She's very self-contained. I've never known what she was thinking or feeling. I used to tell myself it didn't really matter, because her mother was pretty much in charge of bringing her up, and I figured she knew best. I mean, I couldn't really argue with the results. Heather gets top grades. She's a wonderful skater and may even go to the Olympics. But now you're telling me she does these mean things to her schoolmates, and I have to admit that I believe you. I don't want to, but I do."

"Maybe you should talk to a counselor," suggested Lucy. "Someone who specializes in adolescent psychology."

"Maybe you're right," said Lenny, picking up his briefcase and sighing. "It never rains, but it pours, right? I mean, here I've lost my wife, and now my daughter is acting up, and the thing that really worries me," he said, staring right into her eyes, "is what will happen to Heather if something happens to me?"

"I don't think you should worry about that," said Lucy. "You look pretty healthy to me."

"It's not my health. It's my freedom," he said, with a little shrug. "I'm a lawyer, I'm trained to consider all the possibilities, and it seems pretty likely that Bar's lawyers are going to try to paint me as the most obvious suspect. The husband always is."

"But you couldn't possibly have done it. You were out in plain view, playing tennis with her, when she was shot."

"Look, all they have to do is create reasonable doubt. They can imply, even speculate, that I hired somebody to kill her, and had the shooter wear a blond wig to throw suspicion on Bar."

"Would that be admissible?"

"No, of course not. But even if the judge tells the jury to disregard it, they'll have heard it, and the media will pick right up on it. And I think Bob must already have been spinning that story to the cops, because I've been asked some pretty strange questions lately by the prosecutors."

"I don't think Bob would do anything like that, but Bar herself suggested that you might be involved in some way when I interviewed her the other day," admitted Lucy.

"She did? God, that woman's a bitch!" He paused. "Are you going to put it in the paper?"

"I don't know," admitted Lucy. "Ted just had me write a short teaser for this week's paper. I'm supposed to write up the interview for next week's paper. But if I do put it in, I would get a response from you so you could deny it. That's standard practice."

"Fair and balanced, right?" he asked sarcastically.

"We try," said Lucy.

"Well, if you really want to be fair and balanced, think about this. Maybe Bart's the one who killed Tina. Maybe he did it to frame his wife. Ever think of that?"

"Not specifically," said Lucy, "but I have heard a theory that you two conspired to kill one wife and frame the other in order to get both of them out of the way."

Lenny's eyes grew big; then he exploded into short, barking laughter. "Small towns, you gotta love them, don't you? Everybody thinks they know everything, and they actually know nothing."

"No conspiracy?"

"I wouldn't give that guy bus fare," said Lenny. "He's an obnoxious, stuck-up bastard, and you can quote me on that, if you want."

"Not really. Ted has a strong desire to stay out of libel court."

"Too bad," said Lenny, resuming his walk to the car. "Because the more I think about it, the more I think that framing his wife for Tina's murder is exactly the sort of weaselly thing Bart Hume would do."

"And why do you think that?" asked Lucy as he opened the rear car door and slid his briefcase inside.

Lenny looked at her as if she were incredibly stupid. "Because with a life sentence, he gets rid of Bar, and there's no question of alimony," he said. It was clearly his last word on the subject. He yanked open the rusted front car door and slid behind the steering wheel and carefully fastened his seatbelt. The car didn't start when he turned the key, however, and Lucy could still hear him attempting to get the engine to turn over when she reached the office.

CHAPTER FIFTEEN

Pulling the door open, Lucy wondered why, all of a sudden, everybody seemed to be fingering Bart as Tina's killer. Was it the Martha Stewart syndrome? Was Bart, the eminent cardiac surgeon, church deacon, and Republican Party stalwart, just too perfect to be true?

Phyllis certainly thought so. She could hardly wait for Lucy to get through the door before she began relating his latest advance to Elfrida.

"You won't believe this," she began, primly pursing her lips. "That Dr. Straight-and-Narrow has some mouth on him. Elfrida called me last night, all upset. Said she couldn't believe what she was hearing, just because she won't put out for him in the storage closet."

"The storage closet?"

"Yeah, he wants to keep it a secret because his girlfriend is real jealous."

Lucy was puzzled. "His girlfriend?"

"Yeah, his receptionist. Amanda Connell."

"Are you telling me that Bart already has a girlfriend, but he still wants to mess around with Elfrida?"

"Right. And Elfrida doesn't want anything to do with him, and that's exactly what she told him, nice and polite, and he started this foulmouthed tirade."

"That doesn't sound like Bart," insisted Lucy. "Are you sure Elfrida isn't exaggerating?"

"Not Elfrida. Say what you will about her morals, but she's painfully honest."

Lucy tended to agree, and she knew that men could be crude, even highly educated professional men. "Okay, so what did he say?"

Phyllis squeezed her lips together. "I can't say."

"Oh, come on," coaxed Lucy. "We're alone, and believe me, I've pretty much heard it all. My husband's in the building trades. My son went to college, and although he didn't get a diploma, he did pick up some interesting language, which he's had the opportunity to refine as a fisherman."

"Oh, I know nothing would offend you," said Phyllis.

"I wouldn't exactly say that," protested Lucy.

"You know what I mean," said Phyllis, with a dismissive flap of her hand. "We're both big girls, right? But Elfrida wouldn't tell me."

"Why not?"

"She said it was so foul, she absolutely could not bring herself to repeat it."

"Elfrida never struck me as particularly prudish," said Lucy. "What could he possibly have said?"

Phyllis shrugged. "Maybe something medical?"

"I guess doctors probably have a different view of bodily functions," speculated Lucy. "There's really no polite way to talk about colon cancer or venereal disease, things like that, but it hardly seems the way to a girl's heart."

Phyllis raised one eyebrow, attempting to adopt a lascivious expression, but only managing to look comical. "Sweetheart, you haven't had a pelvic exam until you've had a Bart Hume pelvic."

"Oh stop!" protested Lucy, grimacing and laughing at the same time. "That's awful."

"Elfrida said it was horrible," said Phyllis. "She's thinking of filing a sexual harassment complaint."

"Really?" asked Lucy, suddenly serious. "How's she going to do that if she can't say the words?"

"She says she'll write them, with blank spaces."

"A sexual harassment complaint is a serious step," said Lucy. "She better think it over. Something like that can backfire."

"That's what I told her," said Phyllis. "You mess with somebody like Dr. Barton Hume at your peril."

"Keep me posted," said Lucy, sitting down at her desk and booting up the computer. "That would be a big story, if she does file a complaint."

"I hadn't thought of that," said Phyllis, reaching for the phone. "I better warn Elfrida. She's a shy thing. I don't think she'd like having her name in the papers."

Lucy bit her tongue, remembering Elfrida's highly public battle with the historical commission when she wanted to paint her house in zebra stripes, arguing that black and white were approved colors. She finally gave up when the commission threatened to impose penalties and fines, but stubbornly flew a zebra design flag from her porch.

Half listening to Phyllis's conversation, she Googled Bart, skipping over the recent news stories about his wife and scrolling down to earlier, pre-murder listings. There were plenty of them. He not only had his own Web site, complete with photos of himself as well as group family photos, but there were also interviews, newspaper and magazine articles citing various awards from political, charitable, and pro-life organizations, and a number of extracts from medical journals in which he was included among a group of contributing scientists. In all, there was nothing to detract from his image as an ideal family man, accomplished professional, and upstanding citizen.

Recalling Bar's suggestion that Tina might have been targeted by an extreme pro-life group, Lucy checked out several of those Web sites and eventually found a hit list of abortion providers. She thought it extremely odd that a group that claimed to be pro-life was advocating murder and was even providing the addresses of clinics and physicians. She was also shocked to see they'd apparently had some success, as red lines had been drawn through several names, indicating successful hits. Tina's name, however, was not on the list.

She was wondering if perhaps there should be some limits on free speech and was closing Google when she noticed Phyllis's voice had become excited, and she began to pay closer attention. "You're kidding!" Phyllis was exclaiming. "I can't believe it."

When she hung up, Lucy couldn't resist. "What can't you believe?"

"What Elfrida told me. She said she called the HR lady at the hospital just to kind of sound her out about what was involved in filing a sexual harassment complaint, and the woman immediately guessed it was Dr. Hume and practically begged Elfrida to come forward, saying that if she did, she was sure there were several other women who would also file complaints."

"I don't understand," said Lucy.

"Well, the HR lady said the others have been afraid to go public, but she thought that if one person would do it, so would the others."

"I can see that," said Lucy, impulsively reaching for the phone and dialing Bart's office. She didn't really expect to speak to him directly, but the receptionist put her call right through, and when Lucy explained she had interviewed Bar at Bob Goodman's request and was writing a story from her point of view, he immediately agreed to see her, suggesting she come around to his house for lunch. "I always eat lunch at home," he told her. "My work is so demanding that I find I need to touch base, so to speak, to keep things in perspective."

The Hume house was one of the immaculately restored sea captain's houses that lined Main Street. A substantial Georgian-style house with two stories, it had a white clapboard front and an imposing front door flanked with sidelights and topped with an oversized pediment. There were two windows with black shutters on either side of the door, and the second story had five windows, to complete the symmetrical design. The roof featured two chimneys, one on either side, and a widow's walk in the center.

Lucy wasn't thinking about eighteenth-century architecture, however, as she rang the bell. She was wondering if she was the fly walking into the seductive spider's sticky parlor.

"Come in, come in," said Bart, greeting her with a big smile and a hearty handshake. Surprisingly enough, he was wearing madras shorts and a Dice-K T-shirt. They were wildly popular, and Lucy knew the Japanese letters on his chest meant "strike out."

"A baseball fan?" she asked, stepping inside.

"Last year's Father's Day present," he said. "Like I told you on the phone, I try to take a break in the middle of the day, if I can. I'm at the hospital early. Then I have office hours in the afternoon and generally something at night. This is the only time I get to myself."

"I'm jealous," said Lucy. "Ted's a slave driver."

"I don't believe that," he said, leading the way to the kitchen. "He's a good guy."

Lucy followed, taking in the gleaming wood floors, the graceful stairway that swirled up the left wall, the polished gilt mirror that hung above an important-looking mahogany sideboard, the Oriental rugs, and the oil paintings of horses and dogs. And that was just the front hall.

"What a lovely house," she said. It wasn't her style, but she had to admit Bar was right. The place sure had class.

"It's not the same without Bar," he said, pushing open the kitchen door. As she expected, the kitchen had been done to death with granite countertops, top-of-the-line stainless appliances, and at least fifty thousand dollars' worth of English-style kitchen cabinets, with plate racks, reeded moldings, and an enormous range hood with an elaborate carved coat of arms that Grinling Gibbons would have envied. The cook, a dark-haired woman who was almost as wide as she was tall, was working silently at the center island, and Lucy wondered if Bar had had her husband's wandering eye in mind when she'd hired her as they seated themselves at an oak trestle table set in a windowed alcove.

"This is very nice," said Lucy, unfolding the plaid cloth napkin and spreading it on her lap. The table was set simply with matching plaid place mats, white plates, greenish glass goblets, old rat-tail silver, and a bouquet of roses.

Bart lowered his head, then raised it to reveal a pained expression. "I feel so guilty, here, with all this, when Bar is stuck in that . . . ," he said, his voice trailing off.

"As jails go, it's not too bad," said Lucy. "Not that that's any comfort, but when I saw her, she seemed to be holding up very well."

"That's my Bar," he said. "She's got true grit. You'll see. She'll be proven innocent. There's no case against her. It's all circumstantial. Whatever the prosecution throws at us, her lawyer will be able to rip it apart." He paused and snapped his fingers. "Hey, chiquita! We haven't got all day here."

Lucy glanced at the cook, who looked as if she hadn't appreciated Bart's comment. "It's almost ready, Dr. Hume," she said, ladling out the soup. "And you know, I asked you to call me Alma, because that's my name."

"Okay, Alma," he said, catching Lucy's eye. "They come. They go. It's easier to call 'em all *chiquita*. It's never been a problem before, but this one is sensitive." He raised his voice as she approached with the bowls of soup. "Hell of a good cook, though. That's why we put up with her."

"Corn chowder, just the way you like it," said Alma, placing the bowls in front of them. She stepped back and stood, her hands folded. "Shall I serve the salad now, or do you want to wait?"

"Better give it to us now. We've got a lot to talk about," said Bart. "And while you're at it, could you be a doll and bring me the Tabasco sauce?"

"Right away," grumbled Alma, bringing over a generous bowl of salad studded with bacon bits, nuts, and dried fruit, as well as a large bottle of Tabasco sauce. Then she withdrew and left them alone. In the distance, Lucy heard a vacuum cleaner start.

"Take the blond hair the witnesses saw," said Bart, adding a generous shake of hot sauce to his soup and resuming his argument. "Could've been a wig. Fingerprints on the gun? It was my wife's gun. Of course, it had her fingerprints. But that doesn't mean she shot it. The shooter could have stolen it."

Lucy listened, savoring the delicious soup before asking, "Was there a theft? Was anything else missing?"

"Not important," said Bart, pausing to slurp some soup. "All we have to establish is reasonable doubt, and the truth is that Bar wasn't feeling good that morning and never left her bed. She was sleeping so soundly that anybody could have sneaked into the house, unnoticed, and taken the gun."

"Where was it kept?" asked Lucy.

"In the shooting gallery. She's got a practice range in the cellar."

"Is that widely known?" asked Lucy.

"Sure. She has friends over for practice shoots. And her coach and, you know, fellow gun-club members, people like that."

"Oh," said Lucy, who couldn't quite equate a home shooting gallery with, say, a pool or tennis court.

Bart seemed to sense her discomfort with the idea. "Look, lots of people have home theaters, right? Or bowling alleys? This is no different. It's good family fun. Even Ashley enjoys firing off a few rounds now and then." He slurped up some soup. "Of course, she's not nearly as good as her mother."

"Sure," said Lucy, who had her doubts about target shooting as a wholesome family activity. "But what about motive? Bar and Tina had a long-standing rivalry. Everybody knew about it. I saw them fighting over a fifty-cent newspaper at the IGA."

"Okay, I'll admit Tina wasn't Bar's favorite person, but that doesn't mean she killed her. In fact, a very clever killer could have taken advantage of that rivalry to frame Bar."

Lucy put down her spoon and took a deep breath, determined to ask the tough question. "Well, that brings me to a question I have to ask you. There are rumors around town, a lot of people are saying, in fact, that maybe you are that clever person who framed Bar."

If Bart was upset by this accusation, he didn't show it. Instead, he calmly tore a piece off his whole-wheat roll and slathered it with butter. "That's ridiculous," he said, popping it in his mouth.

"Of course, it's nonsense, but people are saying that you did it to get rid of Bar, that a life sentence gets her out of your way without the embarrassment of divorce and the cost of alimony." She paused, stirring her soup with the spoon.

"You could say the same about half the married people in the state," said Bart. Lucy suspected he was furious with her, but he forced his mouth into a smile and picked up his spoon. "It just goes to show that most people are fools and will say anything. I've even heard people speculate that Lenny hired a killer to get rid of Tina." He scooped up a spoonful of soup and slurped it off his spoon, swallowed noisily, and went back for more.

"I suppose that's it," agreed Lucy, with a dismissive shrug. "People will say anything. I've even heard rumors that you and Bar weren't very happy and that you're known at the hospital as a flirt."

Bart got his mouthful of soup down with difficulty and took a drink of water. "This is the sort of thing we doctors have to deal with all the time," he said. "We are surrounded by women, and they all think they're irresistible. As if I'd even look at any woman other than Bar — except in a professional capacity, of course."

"Of course," said Lucy.

He leveled his gaze and looked her straight in the eye, reminding Lucy of a politician running for office. "Bar and I have been married for more than twenty years," he said, "and I hope we'll make fifty, just like my folks did last year. That's how I feel about my wife. I want her out of jail and home, here, where she belongs."

Lucy nodded as she set her soup bowl aside and helped herself to salad. "I imagine Ashley must miss her mother very much."

Bart had taken another big bite of crusty roll and was chewing. He shoved a forkful of salad in his mouth before answering. "Of course, she does," he said, giving Lucy a view of half-chewed lettuce and bread. "A girl her age needs her mother. The timing couldn't be worse, since this is the year that really counts with colleges. But Ashley's well aware that she can't afford to let her grades slip. Or her tennis. There's a good chance she'll get the state championship again this year, which would look great on her applications."

Lucy had a sudden surge of sympathy for Ashley, who was under so much pressure to succeed, despite the fact that her mother was away in jail and had been charged with murder. "Does she have much contact with her mother?"

"Only by phone. We, Bar and I, decided it would be too upsetting for her to visit her mother in jail."

"I can understand that," said Lucy, who really didn't. It seemed to her that it might be a relief to Ashley to see that her mother was okay, even if she was in jail. In fact, considering the circumstances, Lucy was almost ready to forgive the girl for being so mean to Sara. She was only a kid, after all, and although she had every material comfort anyone could want, she didn't seem to get the unqualified love from her parents that she needed.

"I hesitate to mention this, but I think you should know," began Lucy, pushing her salad around her plate with a fork, "Ashley and Heather have been terrorizing other kids at school."

Bart was on it in a flash. "What do you mean?"

"They've started rumors. They send nasty text messages. . . ."

Bart interrupted. "I'd believe that of Heather, considering the way she's been brought up, but not my Ashley."

Lucy straightened her back; her heart was pounding. "Your Ashley even used her cell phone in the gym locker room to take a picture of one girl in her underwear, and sent it to the boys on the football team."

Bart shrugged and grinned. "I bet the boys loved it."

"That doesn't excuse it," said Lucy, finding his attitude shockingly offensive. "It was a violation of privacy. Of trust."

"She'll get over it," he replied, with a shrug. "No blood was shed, right?"

"The girl was embarrassed. Her feelings were hurt."

"It's just part of growing up. We all go through it. This is nothing like the stuff I had to go through in prep school, let me tell you. Now that was rough."

"I don't understand," said Lucy. "If you suffered so much, why don't you want to stop this sort of thing? By tolerating this behavior, you're actually encouraging it."

"Me? How can I stop it? It's the way of the world," he said, putting his napkin down beside his plate. "Sorry, but I've got to run. I've got office hours in half an hour."

"Thanks for the lunch," said Lucy, reaching for her napkin and starting to rise.

"No, no. Stay as long as you like. Finish your lunch."

"Well, thank you," said Lucy, picking up her fork. "This salad really is delicious, and so was the soup."

"I'll be sure to tell *chiquita,*" said Bart, taking his leave. A few minutes later she heard the crunch of his tires as his big Mercedes rolled down the pristine oystershell drive.

Lucy sat there alone, enjoying the rare

moment of quiet. There was no sound in the kitchen except for the ticking of the clock and the chirping of birds outside. The huge stainless-steel refrigerator clicked on and hummed a bit, then stopped. She savored each bite of salad, chasing down the last bit of walnut, the final dried cranberry. She had just finished but was lingering, hoping Alma might return so she could ask a few discreet questions, when Ashley wandered in.

"Who are you?" she demanded, surprised.

"I'm Lucy Stone, from the *Pennysaver*. I was interviewing your father. He left for work before I finished my lunch, so he told me to stay."

"Oh." Ashley fingered her hair, which looked as if it needed a deep conditioning. In fact, it seemed to Lucy that the girl could use a decent meal. Her legs were little more than sticks, with round, bulging knees, and her collarbone poked up sharply beneath her pink Juicy Couture shirt. "I guess that's okay then," she said, taking a glass out of a cabinet and filling it from the water dispenser on the refrigerator door.

"I saw your mother the other day," said Lucy. "She's doing okay."

"She's in jail," said Ashley.

"Yeah, but she's doing all right. I know

she'd want you to know that."

Ashley gave her a sideways look. "Well, thanks for the info."

"Listen, I know you're going through a lot right now, but there's no point making other people's lives miserable."

Ashley stared at her, scowling. "What are you talking about?"

"My daughter. Sara Stone. You've been playing some mean tricks on her."

"Did she tell you that?" demanded Ashley, angrily.

"That's not the point," said Lucy. She was angry herself but trying not to show it. "The point is that I know what you've been doing, and it has to stop."

"Whatever Sara's told you, she's lying. She just wants to get me in trouble. She's the one who's playing tricks, trying to make me look bad."

"I don't think so," said Lucy. She was shocked at Ashley's reaction. She'd expected contrition, maybe even an apology, but not this outright defiance.

"Look," said Ashley, pulling herself up to her full height and staring at Lucy with enormous, blazing eyes, "maybe my dad said you could stay, but you've finished your lunch, and it's time for you to go."

"Okay," said Lucy, picking up her bag.

She paused at the door. "Tell Alma the lunch was delicious."

"Whatever," said Ashley, slamming the door behind her.

CHAPTER SIXTEEN

The walk back to the office passed in a flash as Lucy replayed the lunch with Bart. This was one guy, she decided, who did not improve upon a closer acquaintance. He claimed to love his wife but hadn't really come up with a convincing denial of the rumors that he was a womanizer. Come to think of it, thought Lucy, if the way he treated Alma was any indication, he was a classic misogynist. He seemed to have absolutely no respect for women, viewing them as little more than beings created for his convenience and sexual gratification.

The lunch had been delicious, the surroundings had been lovely, but somehow the whole experience had made Lucy feel a bit dirty. In most interviews she was able to establish a rapport with the subject, and she usually felt that she got to know the person in some way, but not with Bart. His desire to control things, to be in charge, got in the way of any real communication. His only interest had been getting her to believe the line he was spinning; there had been no real exchange at all.

And what about Ashley? She seemed to be a chip off the old block, every bit as cold and callous as her father. Or was it just a front? Was she suffering all the insecurities normal to adolescence, compounded by grief and shame over her mother's situation, but skilled at hiding her anxiety?

The one conclusion that Lucy drew from her contact with the Humes was that they were not an appealing group. But if she were to choose, she decided as she opened the office door and set the little bell to jingling, Bart was the rottenest apple in that particular barrel. She suspected he might well be capable of anything as long as it seemed to be in his interest.

"So what did you think of the doctor?" asked Phyllis. "Did he come on to you?"

"No," said Lucy. "He said he hopes to celebrate his fiftieth wedding anniversary with Bar."

"I guess you're not his type," said Phyllis, handing her a stack of press releases.

Lucy sighed and settled herself at her desk, prepared for a slow Thursday afternoon since Ted was still away at the conference. She plugged away at the listings, routine work that involved reading press releases announcing various events, such as club meetings and ham and bean suppers, sorting them by date, and condensing the relevant details into a concise format for the Around Town section of the paper. Lucy usually enjoyed working on listings, because it offered a break from the more demanding task of reporting, but today she would have preferred something that involved more concentration. The listings were leaving entirely too many brain cells with nothing to do except worry about Sara.

It was ridiculous, she told herself as she typed in the ticket price for the Sweet Adelines concert. School was supposed to be about learning, wasn't it? About getting kids ready for college, right? And Sara had always had good grades; she was right up there in the top 10 percent. So why was she worried about this social nonsense? What did it matter if Heather and Ashley were spreading false rumors? Sara's friends would know it was all lies. And as for the photo they'd circulated of Sara in her underwear, well, truth be told, the sports bra and cotton panties she wore on gym days covered a lot more skin than the bikini she'd worn last summer. And as for that rumor about Sara having sex with Chad, Lucy refused to believe it.

Come to think of it, she told herself as she moved on to the police department's lost property sale, there was a real possibility that she was a lot more concerned about Ashley and Heather's mean tricks than Sara was. As a mother, she instinctively wanted to protect her daughter, but Sara seemed quite capable of taking care of herself. She had good friends, her teachers liked her, and she was surely better liked than Ashley and Heather, with their mean tricks — which was exactly what Lucy discovered when she got home.

She had barely gotten through the door when Sara jumped on her with exciting news. "Guess what, Mom? Chad asked me to go to the movies with him on Friday night! It's a date, a real date!"

Lucy didn't share her daughter's enthusiasm. The well-supervised prom was one thing; a date with an older boy who had a driver's license was another thing entirely. Lucy didn't like the idea one bit. "Last I heard he was in jail," she said. "What happened?"

"Bail, Mom. And he says his lawyer is confident they can't make the charges stick.

He was just defending himself from Tommy."

"That's a bit of a reach, isn't it? After all, Tommy ended up in the hospital."

"He was in school today, with a broken finger, which serves him right, if you ask me. So what about the date?"

Lucy didn't want to handle this one. "You'll have to get permission from your father."

Sara's jaw dropped. "What?"

"You heard me. You need to check with your father. After all, Chad's quite a bit older than you are, and he has a driver's license. I'm not sure we want you to be in a situation like that. Maybe we could drive you to the movie, and you could meet him there."

"Mom! That's crazy! It's embarrassing!"

"Better embarrassed than dead," said Lucy as news footage of crashed cars ran through her mind. Every month, at least, it seemed some teen driver in the region managed to lose control and crash into a tree or stone wall. And often as not, the driver wasn't alone but had a car full of friends. It was practically an epidemic. "Besides, you're only fourteen. I'm not convinced that's old enough for dating."

"I'm almost fifteen! And it's a group date,

Mom. A whole crowd is going."

"That's supposed to make me feel better?" asked Lucy.

"Aw, Mom. There's safety in numbers, right?"

"Have you ever heard the phrase 'group pressure'?"

"You're so mean!" exclaimed Sara, storming out of the kitchen.

"Goes with the territory," muttered Lucy, opening the refrigerator and pulling out the chicken breasts she planned to cook for dinner.

When Bill came home, he didn't offer the support Lucy was looking for. "I don't get it," he said, sitting down at the kitchen table and popping the tab on a can of beer. "You'll spend hundreds of dollars on a fancy dress so she can go to the prom, but you don't want her to go to the movies?"

"It's different," began Lucy, sensing she wasn't entirely rational on this subject. "The prom is supervised. They're all dressed up. They're on their best behavior. The movies, on the other hand, well . . . It's dark and anything can happen."

"But you said she's going with a group."

Lucy wanted to scream. "Weren't you ever at a party where there was group pressure to do something you didn't want to do, like, say, play spin the bottle?"

Bill took a swallow and set the can down. "Nope. I always wanted to play spin the bottle."

"My point exactly!" she crowed, triumphant. "Do you want your daughter playing spin the bottle?"

"In a movie theater?"

"You know what I mean!" she exclaimed, disgusted. "She's fourteen years old. This Chad is seventeen. That's a big difference."

"Face it, Lucy," said Bill. "She's growing up. Sooner or later she's going to get kissed. You're going to have to let go and trust her to make the right decisions. I don't have any problem with a group movie date."

"You're the best dad a girl ever had!" exclaimed Sara, bursting through the door to the kitchen. "See, Mom. Dad understands."

"Not so fast, young lady," said Bill, irritated by her eavesdropping. "There are some conditions. I want this young man to pick you up at the house, and I want him to come into the house to meet me. None of this honking the horn and you flying off without saying good-bye."

"No problem," said Sara.

"And don't eavesdrop when your mother and I are having a conversation," added Bill.

"I'm sorry." Sara lowered her head in an effort to look contrite.

Lucy wasn't convinced. She was furious with them both but knew when she was beat. "Supper's ready," she said, stabbing a chicken breast with a fork and transferring it from the skillet to a platter. "Sara, pour the milk."

Ted was due back at the office Friday morning but came in late due to a news conference at the county courthouse in Gilead, announcing that progress had been made in the Corinne Appleton case. The details, as he recounted them, were enough to give any parent pause.

"You remember how that bird-watcher found those bones?" he began. "Well, the crime lab techs found some tire tracks nearby, and they were able to match them to a van belonging to a guy they'd questioned back when Corinne disappeared, a video store manager over in Lodi. Name is Martin Wicker."

"This guy's been there the whole time?" Lodi, Lucy knew, was just a short distance from Shiloh and served as a commercial center for the area, with several bank branches, a supermarket, and a strip mall with several small shops, including the video store.

"Yeah," said Ted. "Wicker was a suspect because witnesses recalled seeing a white van in town that morning, but the cops didn't have anything else on him until they made the match to the tires," said Ted.

"I suppose Corinne knew him. She'd been to the store?" asked Phyllis.

"You said it. Apparently, he made a point of being real nice to the kids. He'd recommend movies and ask them how they liked them, stuff like that."

Phyllis frowned. "So when he pulled up in his van . . ."

"She recognized him. She thought he was a nice guy, and she hopped right in," said Ted.

"That was pretty stupid," said Phyllis.

"He tricked her," said Ted. "He made a full confession. He was apparently quite proud of himself. He told her he'd seen a little boy wearing a rec department T-shirt, stumbling along the sidewalk, and crying a few blocks back. He thought he must've skinned his knee or something and offered to take her to him and bring them both back to the park, where she could give him first aid. She felt responsible for the kid, since she was a rec program counselor, and she recognized Wicker. She thought he was okay. Better than okay, a really nice guy."

"This is seriously creepy," said Lucy, thinking of how Sara had been flitting around town in her bikini. Would she have fallen for a trick like that?

"What happened after that?" asked Phyllis.

"There was no kid, of course, but he told her the kid must have decided to go back home. It was still about a half hour before the rec program was supposed to start, so he suggested they go for a little ride. He knew where there were some rare trillium flowers blooming in the woods, not far from the road at all. She hesitated, he said, but agreed as long as he promised to get her back to the park in time. Of course, he took her a good ways up the mountain road, and when she began to protest that she'd be late, there was really nothing she could do, short of jumping out of the van. When they finally stopped, she was pretty upset, crying, and he took that as an opportunity to hug her. She began to struggle, and he says that's when he accidentally killed her, but the cops don't buy it." Ted paused. "There's evidence she was in his apartment."

"Oh my gosh," said Lucy, horrified.

"It gets worse," continued Ted. "They've got his van, and they found duct tape and plastic bags and a shovel in it."

"When they arrested him?" asked Lucy. "How come they didn't find that stuff before?"

"The stuff wasn't there when they first checked the van." Ted paused. "They think he was getting ready to do it again."

Lucy's stomach lurched; she felt sick. "You mean he was out there, prowling for another young girl?"

Ted nodded. "This is his mug shot, if you're interested." He pulled a Xerox copy of the photo out of his briefcase. It showed an ordinary-looking guy, about thirty years old, with glasses and a standard barbershop haircut. In profile he had a slightly receding chin.

"He doesn't look like a murderer," said Lucy, "but they never do, do they?"

"Well, if you ask me, when they catch him, they should just skip the trial and hang him," declared Phyllis.

"Amen," said Lucy.

Daughters were certainly a trial, thought Lucy as she helped Sara primp for her date. They wanted to be pretty and attractive, and you helped them with your motherly advice — "Try holding the blow-dryer like this" and "The pink lipstick is prettier" —

and then you had to hope they weren't going to attract the wrong sort of attention. As she fussed over Sara's hair, she wondered if Corinne's mother had given Corinne advice on her appearance that fatal morning. *Wear the blue shirt, honey. It matches your eyes.*

"You've got your cell phone, right?" Lucy asked.

"Sure, Mom."

"Well, don't hesitate to call if you feel the least bit uncomfortable."

"Mom," protested Sara, her cheeks turning pink. "He isn't going to rape me or anything."

"I certainly hope not, but date rape does happen. Boys have a different physiology."

"What's physiology?" asked Zoe, who was watching the process with fascination.

"Nothing you need to worry about," said Lucy, bending low and whispering in Sara's ear. "Remember, you don't need to do anything you don't feel right about."

"Mom!" exclaimed Sara. "Stop! It's a movie. That's all."

A dark suspicion suddenly formed in Lucy's mind. "What movie?"

"I'm not sure. Some superhero thing, from a comic book."

"Oh," said Lucy, but her relief was short-lived. The sound of the doorbell sent her scurrying into the upstairs hall, where she could hear Bill's conversation with Chad.

"How ya doin'?" he was saying.

"Good," said Chad.

Lucy waited for Bill to begin reading him the riot act, but she was disappointed.

"You're missing a good game," said Bill. "Dice-K is pitching tonight."

"Yeah," agreed Chad. "I'll see it later. We've got DVR."

Come on, Bill, Lucy was saying to herself. *Tell him she has to be home by eleven, no exceptions.*

"So how does DVR work?" asked Bill.

Lucy wanted to scream.

"It's with the cable company. You can program the cable box to record games, whatever you want. It's pretty cool."

Ask him about the movie, she muttered to herself. *What's the rating?*

"Is it complicated?" asked Bill.

"Nah," said Chad. "My mom can do it."

For pete's sake, she fumed. *Remind him to drive carefully.*

"I'll have to look into it," said Bill as Sara appeared at the top of the stairs.

Observing their reaction as they watched Sara descend, Lucy was convinced she knew just how Dr. Frankenstein felt. She had created a monstrously attractive girl. They were both speechless, gazing upward, as this slender yet buxom blond vision in skinny jeans and a halter top bounced down, holding a sweater over her arm.

"Hi, Chad," Sara said coolly. "Bye, Dad. Bye, Mom," she added, and with a toss of her ponytail, she was gone.

"Damn, Lucy," exclaimed Bill as the door closed behind them. "You didn't tell me she was going to look like that."

"What? You see her every day. A little lip gloss and a few curlers don't make that much difference."

He stood in the hallway, clearly dismayed, as Chad gunned the motor of his sports car and shot down the driveway, then squealed the brakes, making the turn onto Red Top Road. "I guess it was the way he looked at her."

Lucy had no pity. "Like she was good enough to eat?" she asked, with a smug smile.

"Don't," he protested, with a small moan. "What's the number for the cable company?"

"It's in the book," said Lucy. "C'mon, Zoe. Let's go visit baby Patrick."

Patrick was having his bath when Lucy and Sara arrived at Toby and Molly's house. The two-month-old was nestled into a contoured baby tub, and Toby was carefully wiping each tiny toe, each little ear, with a miniature washcloth. Patrick wasn't exactly loving it, but he wasn't crying when Toby squeezed the cloth and dribbled warm water on his tummy.

"All finished," said Toby, lifting the slippery little newt out of the water and handing him to Lucy, who wrapped him in a fluffy towel. She pressed her nose against his nearly bald head, sniffing the sweet smell of baby shampoo.

"Can I put on his diaper?" asked Zoe.

"Sure," laughed Molly. "And his jammies, too. Everything's on the changing table."

Soon a sweet and clean Patrick was nestled at his mother's breast, taking his bedtime meal, and Toby was pulling board games out of the hall closet.

"Trivial Pursuit?" suggested Toby.

"Takes too long," said Molly. "I want to get some sleep before he wakes up for his midnight feeding. And the two o'clock. And the four."

Lucy remembered what it was like and gave her a sympathetic smile.

"Scrabble?" asked Toby.

"Mom always wins," said Zoe.

"Clue?" he proposed.

"We haven't played that in a long time," said Molly.

"Let's go for it," said Toby, spreading out the board on the coffee table. Soon the cards were distributed, and they were advancing around the board.

As they played, Lucy wished real life was as neat as the game. There were no messy emotions in Clue: it didn't matter if it was Professor Plum in the library, with a lead pipe, or Miss Scarlet in the hall, with a rope. Nobody shed a tear; no emotions were involved. These crimes had no consequences, and solving them was simply a matter of elimination and a lucky guess or two. The game was over in an hour or so; it didn't take more than a year to solve these crimes, a year in which Corinne's grieving parents struggled to simply get through every day.

"Your turn, Mom," said Toby.

"Right," said Lucy, picking a card. "Okay. I'm guessing it's Colonel Mustard in the dining room, with a candlestick."

Toby handed her the envelope, and she pulled out the three cards. "Ha! I was right," she said, displaying them.

"How'd you do it?" demanded Zoe.

"Just a hunch," Lucy said, thinking of Tina's murder. If only solving it was as simple as playing Clue. She knew it was on the tennis court, with a gun, but who did it? The lawyer, the doctor, or the expert markswoman?

CHAPTER SEVENTEEN

The phone on the kitchen wall was ringing when Lucy and Zoe returned home. Bill, who had cranked the stereo up to maximum volume and was playing his old Neil Young records in the family room, hadn't heard it.

"Hello," said Lucy, pressing the receiver to her ear. All she could make out through Neil's guitar licks was a series of squeaks. "Hold on. I can't hear," she said, turning to Zoe. "Ask Daddy to turn down the music." A few seconds later, rock and roll didn't die, but Neil became somewhat subdued.

"Okay. I can hear you now," she said, but all she heard was gulps and sobs. "Sara?" she guessed, leaping into panic mode. "What's the matter?"

"Ma . . . Ma . . . oh, Mo-o-om," wailed Sara.

"Whatever it is, it's all right," said Lucy, her heart racing. "We'll come get you. Where are you?"

Sara's voice was small, punctuated with sobs. "I'm in jail."

When Lucy and Bill got to the police station, they weren't alone. A number of parents were standing awkwardly in the entry area. Some looked as if they'd risen from their beds and thrown on some clothes; others were dressed for an evening out. They all shared the same expression, a mixture of embarrassment and anger.

The door leading to the interior of the station opened, and Dot's oldest son, Chief Kirwan, appeared. He was young for the job, a rising star. A shining beacon of responsibility, a follower of the straight and narrow path, a law-and-order man. Until now, that had never bothered Lucy.

"When can I see my kid?" demanded one father, a burly guy with a three-day stubble, plaid pajama bottoms, and a Red Sox sweatshirt.

"I know you're anxious about your children," said the chief. "I assume you're all here because you received phone calls?"

They all nodded.

"We'll deal with each case individually, on an alphabetical basis," said the chief. "That way we can protect your child's right to privacy." He paused. "But first, I have some general information for you. At around twenty hundred hours, we received a noise complaint from a Shore Road resident. An officer was sent to investigate, and he found a number of cars parked in the Audubon preserve parking lot and heard loud music and voices emanating from an abandoned cabin adjacent to the preserve. He also found discarded packaging from alcoholic beverages."

Lucy's and Bill's eyes met. Lucy was biting her lip; Bill's jaw had tightened, and a vein in his temple was throbbing.

"The officer called for additional units, and thirteen individuals, ranging in age from fourteen to seventeen years of age, were subsequently arrested on charges of underage drinking, noise violations, trespassing, littering, and violating the open burning bylaw."

"Trespassing?" inquired one mother, dressed in high heels, a little black dress, and pearls.

The chief nodded. "The Audubon preserve is closed from eight p.m. to five a.m. They were parked illegally. The cabin is also on posted property."

"Oh," said the woman, squeezing her clutch purse so tightly that her knuckles were white.

"Okay, let's get started," said the chief, consulting a clipboard. "Aronson."

"Here," answered a heavyset man with a dark five o'-clock shadow. Sighing, he followed the chief through the door.

"Looks like it's going to be a long night," said Lucy, settling her bottom against the wall.

"Humph," was all Bill said.

The little sympathy Lucy had for Sara evaporated when she was finally reunited with her daughter. Sara stank of booze, her hair was a tangled mess studded with dried leaves, and her clothes were stained with soot from the illegal campfire.

"What were you thinking?" Lucy demanded as they finally left the police station and got in the car.

"Rotten cops," declared Sara. "We were just having fun."

"You were breaking the law," said Lucy.

"Several laws," added Bill.

"We weren't hurting anybody," insisted Sara, sullenly.

"You were making enough noise that somebody complained," said Lucy. "And what if the fire had gotten out of control? And how were you going to get home? Was there a designated driver, or was everybody drinking?"

Sara stared out the window.

"Was everybody drinking? Answer your mother, Sara," said Bill.

"Everybody. But it was only beer. You can't get drunk on beer."

Sara herself provided evidence to the contrary. Her mood improved as they drove along, and she was feeling no pain when they pulled into the driveway. "Whee," she sang out as Bill made the turn. "Home at last! I love you, house! I love you, Mom. You too, Dad. Oh, here's Libby. I love you, Libby. You're the best dog ever."

"What's the matter with her?" asked Zoe, who had been waiting for them.

"She's drunk. It's not a pretty sight, is it?" demanded Lucy.

"She seems nicer than usual," said Zoe as her sister engulfed her in a hug. "Ugh. You stink!" she protested, struggling to extricate herself.

"It's late, Zoe. Time for you to be in bed," said Lucy.

Casting a reproachful look over her shoulder, Zoe began climbing the stairs.

"I'll make coffee," said Bill.

"I'll get the shower running," said Lucy.

"I want to dance!" proclaimed Sara.

■ ■ ■ ■

Sara didn't want to dance the next morning.

"I feel sick," she moaned when her mother met her outside the bathroom. "And my head aches."

"The wages of sin," said Lucy.

"What?"

"Otherwise known as a hangover," said Lucy.

"I want to die," said Sara.

"Definitely a hangover," said Bill.

"Scrambled eggs for breakfast?" asked Lucy, brightly.

"I'm going to be sick," said Sara, disappearing into the bathroom.

When she finally emerged, Lucy had aspirin and coffee ready. Bill was also ready, with an ultimatum.

"I'm very disappointed in you, Sara," he began. "Your mother didn't want you to go out last night, and it seems she was right. I thought you were mature enough to behave responsibly, but I was wrong."

"I'm sorry, Dad," said Sara, her head bowed and her eyes cast down.

"Sorry isn't good enough," said Bill. "I'm having serious doubts about letting you go to the prom."

Sara's head snapped up. "Dad! You wouldn't!"

Bill nodded gravely. "Don't test me," he warned. "That dress is returnable."

"Don't I deserve a second chance?" begged Sara, using her sweetest voice.

"We'll see," said Bill. "But for now, you're grounded."

Slowly, painfully, Sara rose to her feet and crossed the family room. Except for the fuzzy slippers, she might have been Marie Antoinette on her way to the guillotine.

"Drama queen," muttered Lucy.

When Monday morning rolled around, Lucy found she was eager to get to work. The weekend had seemed endless, with Sara moping about the house and Bill's simmering anger. Even the dog had seemed on edge, unable to settle down and pacing from room to room, nails clicking on the wood floors.

But the short ride to the office wasn't the peaceful interlude she had hoped for. She had no sooner turned off Red Top Road when she heard sirens, lots of sirens. When it became clear that one of the sirens was from an ambulance, which was rapidly gaining on her, she pulled off the road, then followed it. She was a reporter, after all, and traffic accidents were news, especially one as serious as this seemed to be.

She didn't have far to go. The crash had taken place just outside town, where Packet Road crossed County Road. There was a stop sign at the intersection, but it seemed the driver of an SUV had missed it and been hit by an oil delivery truck. The scene was a smelly mess. The oil truck was lying on its side, leaking stinking fuel. The SUV seemed to have exploded on impact; little could be seen except the crumpled frame, where firemen and EMTs were working to free the trapped driver. Debris was everywhere: bits of insulation, broken glass, a tire, soda cans, and fast-food wrappers, all blowing in the breeze.

Lucy parked on the side of the road and got out, surveying the scene before reaching for her camera and snapping photos. It was easier to deal with the accident by reducing it in size, framing it with her camera's view-finder. Stumbling, she lowered the camera and looked down, discovering she'd become entangled with the strap of a woman's handbag. It struck her as incredibly poi-gnant, this intimately personal item lying there in the middle of the road. She bent and picked it up. A folded piece of paper fell out, and Lucy also retrieved that. It was a notice from the school nurse, addressed to Mrs. Amanda Connell, advising her that her son, Matthew, grade four, had failed an eye exam and should be seen by an optometrist. Lucy slipped it back inside the handbag, which she took over to the nearest cop, Officer Barney Culpepper, who was directing traffic around the scene.

"Thanks, Lucy," he said, carefully placing it by his feet as he held up his hand for a FedEx truck to stop so the ambulance could go by. It was soon screaming down the road at top speed, with lights flashing, and Barney waved the FedEx truck on. "Terrible thing," he said, shaking his head and making his jowls quiver.

"Two victims?"

"Yeah, both drivers. Thank God they were alone."

"Yeah. The SUV driver is a mother. Amanda Connell. There was a note from the school that fell out of her purse."

"Not that nice lady who works for Dr. Hume?" said Barney, shaking his head.

Lucy felt as if bells and whistles and flashing lights were going off in her head. This couldn't be a coincidence, could it? How come, all of a sudden, two of the most important women in Dr. Bart's life were in trouble?

Barney was still talking about how Doc Ryder had sent him to see Dr. Hume a couple of months ago because he had high blood pressure, and how nervous he'd been about seeing a specialist, a surgeon, but Amanda Connell had talked to him and asked about the weather before she took his blood pressure, and it turned out that he only had to take pills, but Lucy was only half listening. She was remembering Phyllis saying something about Dr. Hume's receptionist, something about him having an affair with her.

Bart's mistress, thought Lucy. *First, his wife goes to jail, and then his mistress has a terrible accident.* "How'd it happen?" she asked.

Barney held up his hand for the second ambulance. "She must've missed the stop sign. I dunno. Doesn't seem likely, but you know how it is. If you follow the same route every morning, you might kinda go on automatic pilot."

"Maybe her brakes were bad," said Lucy.

"There's no hill or anything, and she was coming off a windy road. Wouldn't have been goin' real fast. You'd think she coulda downshifted or something." He stared at the wreckage. "She musta been goin' awful fast. Doesn't seem like her."

"Maybe somebody tampered with her car," suggested Lucy.

"That'd explain the accident," said Barney. "But who'd do a thing like that?"

Who indeed? wondered Lucy as she sat down at her desk to write up the story. The first call she made was to Bart's office, but there was no answer. The hospital wasn't forthcoming, either, refusing to release any information. She tried the fire station, using the business number, and got Dot Kirwan's youngest daughter, Bobbi.

"How's the baby?" asked Lucy, who knew Bobbi had delivered around the same time as Molly. They'd been in childbirth classes together.

"She's great — almost twelve pounds already — and she sleeps through the night," bragged Bobbi. "How's little Patrick?"

"Adorable," said Lucy, unwilling to admit that he was a bit of a fussbudget. "We're all crazy about him."

"Wouldn't it be great if you could keep 'em little?" asked Bobbi.

"It sure would," agreed Lucy, thinking of Sara's weekend adventure. "Listen, Bobbi, I wondered if you heard anything about the two accident victims this morning? Do you know their conditions?"

"Not officially," she said, "but the truck driver seemed to have hurt his back or shoulder, something along those lines. Not life threatening."

"What about the woman in the SUV?" asked Lucy.

"The guys didn't think she was going to make it. She had a lot of internal bleeding. It's a shame."

Lucy was silent for a moment, digesting this information. "Any ideas how it happened?"

"Not really. The state police will investigate if it's a fatal."

"Well, thanks," said Lucy. "Give the baby a hug for me."

"Roger, wilco," said Bobbi.

Sighing, Lucy returned to her keyboard, but with nothing to go on but hearsay, there was little she could do except outline the story. That wasn't a problem: the deadline wasn't until noon Wednesday, so she had plenty of time to gather official quotes and fill in the details. She did what she could, then closed the file and turned to the ever-present listings, but her mind kept straying back to the accident. She kept trying to reach Bart, but there was no answer at home, and when she called his office, her call was switched to the answering service, where the operator finally lost patience with her.

"Believe me, I'll make sure the doctor gets your message as soon as he calls in," she said. "There's no need to keep calling."

Lucy knew she was right, but it was like an itch she couldn't scratch. She finally decided to call Bob Goodman, on the off chance he had a way to contact Bart.

Bob had heard about the accident, he said, and had been trying to contact Bart, too, but with no luck. "Poor guy can't catch a break," he said. "First, his wife is charged with murder, and now his nurse is gone. Talk about bad luck."

"Yeah," said Lucy, ending the call. She was beginning to suspect it wasn't just bad luck. "Hey, Phyllis," she said, swiveling in her chair. "Doesn't Elfrida have a kid in fourth grade?"

"Yup. Justin."

"Does he know Matthew Connell?"

"Mattie's his best friend."

"So Elfrida knows his mom?"

"Kinda sorta. Amanda's got attitude. Thinks she's better than just about everybody."

"But she overlooks Elfrida's reputation

266

and lets Mattie play with Justin?"

"Yeah. She's a single, working mom. She'd probably let him play with the spawn of Satan, just to get him somewhere after school."

Lucy nodded. "Didn't you say something the other day about the doctor and his receptionist being an item?"

Phyllis smirked. "Like I said, she's a single mom. She's available."

Lucy's computer chimed, notifying her that an e-mail message from the state police public relations department had arrived. She opened it and learned that the department was investigating a fatal accident that had taken the life of Amanda Connell, thirty-one, of Tinker's Cove.

"She's not available anymore," she said. "Amanda's dead."

CHAPTER EIGHTEEN

It was quiet in the office, except for the tick of the antique wall clock, which had hung there for more than one hundred years, since the days of the old *Courier & Advertiser,* counting down the hours and minutes to thousands of deadlines.

Finally, Phyllis spoke. "I better call Elfie, let her know what happened." Lucy listened as Phyllis punched in the numbers and broke the news; she heard Elfrida's shriek from all the way across the room. When she hung up, Phyllis had plenty to report.

"Elfie couldn't believe it. She said Amanda was a really cautious driver, wouldn't even start the car until everybody was buckled in, never exceeded the speed limit, and counted to three at stop signs."

"Barney couldn't understand it, either," said Lucy. "Packet Road is so twisty that he didn't see how she could have gotten up much speed. His theory was that she might have zoned out because she made the same drive every morning, but even so, he didn't see how she could have gotten up so much speed. He thought her brakes must've failed."

"Not likely. Elfie says Amanda was fanatical about following the recommended service schedule. She changed her oil every three thousand miles, got the tires rotated frequently, and got the car inspected a month before her sticker expired."

Lucy was silent, thinking over this new information, which seemed to confirm her suspicion that the accident wasn't an accident.

"I can read your mind, Lucy Stone," said Phyllis, pointing an apricot-tipped finger at her. "You think there's something fishy about that accident."

"Well," said Lucy. "What if Amanda somehow knew Bart killed Tina in order to get his wife sent to jail? What if she thought she was going to be the next Mrs. Bart Hume, only to discover that Dr. Bart Hume had no intention of marrying her? What if she threatened to go to the police? What do you think?"

"I think that's a whole lot of what-ifs," said Phyllis.

"I know," admitted Lucy, "but somehow

it feels right."

"Sounds like a Lifetime movie to me," said Phyllis. "And what about his daughter? Even if he manages to get rid of Bar, he's still stuck with a teenager."

What about his daughter? Lucy remembered what Sue Finch had said about how controlling Bart was with Ashley. "Almost sexual," was how Sue had described it. And Lucy knew from personal experience that Bart was a creep. But could he possibly be involved in an incestuous relationship with his daughter? These things happened; Lucy knew that. She'd heard about it on *Oprah* and she'd even covered a case or two in Tinker's Cove, but those cases had involved troubled, poverty-stricken families with a host of problems. Still, the social worker she'd interviewed had stressed that incest, like wife abuse, crossed all social strata. "You just don't hear about the rich ones, because they can hide it better," she'd said.

"You're awful quiet," declared Phyllis. "What are you thinking?"

"I'm wondering why men are so icky," said Lucy.

"Now, now, they're not all bad. Take Wilf, for instance. He's a real gentleman," said Phyllis as the phone rang. "It's for you," she said, transferring the call to Lucy's extension.

It was the high school attendance officer. *What now?* Lucy braced herself for more bad news.

"I'm calling to let you know that your daughter, Sara Stone, was reported present by her homeroom teacher, and she attended her first two classes but was absent for period three."

"There must be some mistake," said Lucy. Sara was a good student; there was no reason for her to cut class.

"Perhaps she had a doctor's appointment or some other reason for early dismissal? Sometimes the kids forget to check out at the attendance office."

"No, nothing like that," said Lucy.

"Well, this will go down as an unexcused absence, and she will have to serve a detention," said the attendance officer.

Lucy was troubled as she hung up the phone. What was going on with this kid? First, she went to a booze party in the woods and got arrested, and now she was cutting classes? When did she stop being a model student and turn into a juvenile delinquent? And if she wasn't at school, where was she? *Not,* Lucy prayed, *with Chad Mackenzie.* She quickly dialed Sara's cell phone, intending to read her the riot act, but got the recording telling her to leave a message.

"Trouble?" asked Phyllis. "You look like a mother cat who lost one of her kittens."

"That's exactly right," said Lucy, shoving back her chair and standing up. "And I'm going to go find her."

"Is that what you want me to tell Ted?" asked Phyllis.

"Tell him whatever you want," said Lucy, losing patience and hurrying out of the office.

But where to start? she wondered as she marched down Main Street to her car. *Chad's house? As good a place as any,* she decided, striding past the hardware store and the post office. It was there that she encountered Lenny, standing by the blue mailbox on the sidewalk, holding his cell phone and looking extremely puzzled.

Before she knew what she was saying, Lucy asked, "Attendance officer?"

He looked up, amazed. "How did you know?"

"Because I just got a call, too. My Sara cut third period."

"So did Heather." He paused. "What do you think is going on? She's never skipped class before."

"Neither has Sara," said Lucy, adding, "And she's not accepting phone calls" when she saw Lenny pushing some buttons on his cell phone.

"Neither is Heather," he said, closing his phone and looking at her with a baffled expression. He gave a great sigh and blinked a few times. "It's times like this that I really miss Tina," he said. "She'd know what to do."

Lucy's heart went out to him. People could say what they might about the simple funeral he'd given Tina; there was no mistaking that this was a man who deeply grieved the loss of his wife. She wanted to reach out and hug him, and was trying to think of a way to comfort him when she had a bright idea. "Well, what would Tina do in this situation? Did anything similar ever come up?"

Lenny thought for a minute. "Yeah, one time Heather said she was going on an overnight with the church youth group. Tina had the idea of taking them pizza for a midnight snack, but when we got to the church, there was no sign of Heather. Tina was furious. She drove right over to Ashley Hume's house, and, lo and behold, there was Heather."

Lucy was puzzled. "Why did she have to

lie about spending the night at Ashley's?"

"Oh, Tina didn't approve of their friendship. It drove her crazy. She couldn't stop them from seeing each other at school, but she forbade any other contact."

Weirder and weirder, thought Lucy. "So do you think we should try Ashley's house?"

"It's as good a place as any to start," he said. "I'll meet you there."

When Lucy got to the Humes' house, Lenny was waiting for her. He'd parked his ancient Volvo in the pristine white oyster-shell driveway and was sitting inside it. The junky car seemed out of place, a blot on the image of perfection presented by the carefully maintained and landscaped mansion. Lucy parked behind it, and they followed the herringbone brick pathway to the back door, where they rang the bell. They could hear it chiming inside, but nobody came to the door, not even Alma. Lucy gave the knob an experimental twist and was surprised when it turned.

"Do you think we should go in?" she asked.

"Absolutely not."

"What if they're in there, overdosed on drugs or something?"

Lenny bristled. "What makes you say a

274

thing like that?"

Lucy stared at him. "Do you read the newspapers? Watch TV?"

"Not much," admitted Lenny.

"Well, take it from me, when kids cut school, it isn't because they want to play croquet."

"Okay," he said. "But we'll just take a quick look and get out."

"Right," said Lucy, pushing the door open and stepping inside the mudroom.

The house seemed empty, quiet except for the distant chime of a grandfather clock. They went from room to room, but there was no sign that anybody was there: no half-drunk glasses, no coffee cups, no scattered newspapers. The television sets were all off, the stereo was quiet, everything was neat and tidy, the beds were made, and the clothes were hung up. Lucy was impressed by Ashley's bedroom — a spacious room done up in pink-flowered chintz — until she realized it was the sort of room mothers and decorators thought teenage girls should like but that they really didn't, preferring instead to experiment with black paint, Day-Glo stickers, and rock star posters. It was neat as a pin, which Lucy also thought atypical. She looked around for a computer but found only a printer, so she concluded that wherever Ashley was, she probably had her laptop with her.

There was a computer in Bart's office; he'd left it on in standby mode. Lucy hit the ENTER button, earning a sharp reproof from Lenny and little else. The files listed were all work related. He had a bunch of unopened e-mails, mostly from pharmaceutical companies, and Lucy figured it wasn't worth the risk of discovery to read them. She scanned his Favorites queue, checking to see if it included some porn sites, but it was empty.

Back outside, she turned to Lenny, who was studying a lilac bush. "Well, it was worth a try," she said.

"Look at this," he said, pointing to a patch of broken branches. "It looks like somebody drove into this bush."

Looking closer, Lucy realized that the bush had taken quite a hit. Not only were several crushed twigs lying on the ground, but the leaves and blooms on several branches were wilting fast, a sure sign that they had been damaged.

The discovery made Lucy uneasy. "What do you think happened?"

"It looks like somebody drove out of here real fast and clipped part of the bush," said Lenny. "That's what it looks like to me."

Lucy had to admit the damaged bush certainly didn't go with the carefully groomed perfection of the landscaping, which seemed to issue a challenge to the boldest weed that it would not be welcome. "That's what I think, too," she said, looking for other signs of disturbance. At the end of the drive, she found a small wooden sign with the house number broken off its stake and lying amid the tulips.

"I bet the girls are on a joyride," said Lenny. "There's an old cabin, a camp, out near the Audubon preserve that the kids use for booze parties. You know where I mean?"

"Unfortunately," said Lucy, "I have heard of the place."

Lucy was backing out of the driveway when she noticed Lenny running after her, waving. She braked and watched as he hurried down the drive. He certainly cut an odd figure, with his mop of curly hair, his mismatched pants and jacket, his heavy tortoiseshell glasses, his argyle socks, and Birkenstock sandals.

"My car won't start," he said, with a shrug, reaching for the door handle.

"Do you want to call triple A or something?"

"No," he said, opening the passenger door

and seating himself beside her. "It's happened before. It'll probably be fine when we get back."

"Okay," said Lucy, shifting into reverse. "You be the navigator."

"It's off Shore Road," he said, fastening the seat belt and settling in for the ride. After a bit, he sighed. "I wouldn't want to be a kid nowadays, that's for sure. They've got it a lot harder than we did."

Lucy didn't agree. She remembered her own teen years as an emotional seesaw between terror and yearning. Terrified of the teachers in her strict all-girls school, she'd put in long hours studying: memorizing French verbs, the classification of species, the philosophical influences that shaped the American Revolution. The words *compare and contrast* still made her heart skip a beat. The few moments she hadn't been studying had been spent yearning, mooning after boys she saw on the subway and wishing she could be like the perfect girls in *Seventeen* magazine.

"I don't think growing up has ever been easy," she said.

"Sure, but now it's harder than ever. These kids are under so much pressure, it's no wonder they need to blow off steam."

"Well, I know one thing that's different.

When I was in high school, my mother knew what I was doing. She knew my friends. I even had to get permission to use the telephone to call them."

"Now they've all got cell phones," said Lenny.

"And we don't know what they're saying to each other, do we? My mother couldn't help overhearing my conversations, because the family phone was on a desk in the front hall."

"Ours was in the kitchen," said Lenny.

"Now there's all this technology that they've mastered and we haven't," said Lucy. "We can't find out what they're up to even if we want to. It's as if they live in an alternate universe. The generation gap is a chasm."

"I never thought of it that way," said Lenny. "Turn here."

Lucy pulled off the road onto a grassy drive that was just wide enough for her car; leafy branches brushed the sides as she crept along the uneven surface. Eventually, the undergrowth parted, and they came to a clearing with a ramshackle old hunting camp and a glittering black Mercedes.

"Bart's car," said Lenny, his face growing red. "If he's messing around with my daughter, I'll kill him!"

Lucy sat, drumming her fingers on the steering wheel. The pieces of the puzzle were beginning to fall into place, and she didn't like the way it was shaping up one bit. "What could he be doing with three young girls?" she asked, thinking out loud.

"Maybe he's making pornographic films. Or maybe he's initiating them into some sort of satanic ritual. Or maybe he's into bondage and stuff. Or group sex. I don't know what he's doing, but I'm going to find out," he said, flinging the car door open.

"No!" hissed Lucy, grabbing his arm. "We need to be cautious here. The whole family has guns. They target shoot for fun."

Lenny pulled out his cell phone. "I'll call the cops!"

"Take it easy," said Lucy, who didn't want Sara involved with the police again if she could avoid it. "Let's find out what we're dealing with here, okay? Then we'll decide what to do."

"Okay." Lenny was off, heading straight for the front door.

"Hold on," called Lucy, running after him. "I think it would be smart to come around from the back, just in case." She began weaving her way through the trees and undergrowth. Lenny followed, moving clumsily and stumbling on stones and roots.

A few minutes later they were standing at the edge of the woods, looking across a stretch of overgrown grass dotted with buttercups, staring at the back wall of the cabin. It was covered in worn plywood siding, broken by a chimney made of round stones and a small square window.

"Let's go fast and stay low," advised Lenny. "Head for the far corner, and use the building as cover."

Lucy looked at him in surprise. "Where'd you learn this stuff?"

Lenny shrugged. "Movies."

"Let's hope it works in real life," said Lucy, hunching over and dashing through the grass. Moments later Lenny joined her, and they stood very still, listening to the muffled sounds coming from the cabin: first, the thumping beat of rock music, then a feminine shriek. Instinctively, Lucy reached for Lenny, restraining him. Together they crept along the wall until they reached the window. It was closed tight and very dirty.

Lucy pressed her finger to her lips, and steadying herself by pressing against the wall with her fingers, she slowly raised herself just high enough to peek over the sill. Lenny did the same, and snatching a quick glimpse, they ducked back down.

Flipping around, Lenny collapsed with his back against the wall, his face white with shock. "Oh my God," he said.

Seeing him sitting there, with tears running down his cheeks, Lucy had the fleeting thought that he looked like one of the shocked and wounded survivors of terrorists' bomb blasts you saw pictured on the evening news.

CHAPTER NINETEEN

Now it was Lucy who had to be restrained. The moment she'd glimpsed Sara, tied to a chair, back-to-back with Bart, who was also bound, she was ready to charge to the rescue. Now it was Lenny who was hesitating. He'd grabbed her by the elbow and wasn't letting go.

"Okay, so we'll call the cops," she said, glaring at him and opening her phone.

"No," he said, squeezing her hand and forcing her to close the phone. "I need a minute. I need to think."

"This is out of control," she hissed. "We have to do something now, before . . ." Her voice trailed off. Before what? Was it really true? Had she seen what she thought she saw? Suddenly everything was topsy-turvy; all her assumptions were wrong. Bart hadn't abducted the girls; Heather and Ashley had abducted *him* . . . and Sara, too. They had taken their victims to the cabin, tied them

together with duct tape, and were torment-
ing them. The likely valedictorian and
salutatorian of Tinker's Cove High School
had put on black raincoats, smeared their
faces with black paint, and transformed
themselves into whirling dervishes, each
holding a disposable lighter in one hand and
a handgun in the other. The were playing a
rap song at top volume on a boom box,
dancing and prancing around Bart and
Sara, flicking the lighters in their faces, and
poking them with the handguns. Bart looked
furious; Sara was terrified.

Hearing a muffled moan when there was
a break in the music, Lucy came to a decision. "We've got to call the cops," she said,
opening her phone.

"No!" hissed Lenny.

"Are you crazy? I don't think we've got
much time here. Those girls are working
themselves into a frenzy. We've got to stop
this before they go too far."

"No," declared Lenny, pulling himself
together. "There's got to be an explanation
for this. Maybe they're making a film. That's
it. They're rehearsing a scene. . . ."

Lucy understood he was in shock, in
denial. Lenny, after all, was the sort of father
who gave his daughter a brand-new Prius
while he drove a broken-down old Volvo.

He'd do anything to protect his child. But this was too much; Ashley and Heather had gone too far. "Let's let the police sort it out," she snapped, hitting the nine.

"No!" Lenny grabbed the phone and snapped it shut. "Do you want them to get in trouble?"

"Give that back!" hissed Lucy, eyes blazing. "What I want is for everybody to get out of this alive. You can think what you want, but I suspect it was the girls who killed Tina. We have to stop them now!"

"That's ridiculous," said Lenny. "My Heather wouldn't do that, and neither would Ashley. Trust me. I know a thing or two about negotiating. We'll go in calmly and assess the situation, and then we'll decide what to do."

"What are you saying? You think we can just walk in there and they'll be glad to see us?"

"They'll be relieved," said Lenny, pulling himself up. "You'll see."

It was then that the first shot was fired.

Lucy ran around the cabin and through the door before she had time to think, knocking Heather off her feet. Ashley, who was on the other side of the room, turned and pressed the barrel of her gun against Sara's head. Lucy froze in place, holding

285

her hands up.

"Put the gun down!" yelled Lenny, appearing in the doorway.

Lucy's eyes were on Sara, who was visibly trembling and whose eyes were enormous over the strip of duct tape that was covering her mouth.

Heather, who was sprawled on the floor, pushed herself up to a sitting position and started rubbing her elbows.

"Get up!" ordered Ashley. "Don't go all soft now. Get the duct tape! Tie them up."

Heather seemed to be having second thoughts. Her bottom lip was quivering, and she was blinking furiously, even as she picked up the gun that had fallen to the floor.

"Heather, honey," pleaded Lenny. "Don't listen to her. Don't make things worse. We can work this out. Everything will be okay. Daddy can fix it. Honest."

Heather sniffled, and her eyes darted between her father and Ashley, finally settling on Ashley. "Remember the plan," said Ashley, perfectly composed, her voice steady. "It's worked so far, hasn't it? Everything will be fine as long as we stick to the plan."

Heather was still wavering, supporting herself with one hand while holding the gun with the other. Ashley was in the power position: she was facing Lenny and Lucy and could fire off two rounds at close range in seconds. Lucy remembered Bart bragging that the whole family, including Ashley, enjoyed target shooting. It wasn't a comforting thought.

"The police are on their way," said Lucy, lying through her teeth. "You can't get away. My car is blocking the road, and I've hidden the keys."

On the floor, Heather whimpered, "Daddy's right, Ashley. He'll fix this. He will. You'll still get into Harvard. They took that other girl who killed her mother."

"Shut up!" ordered Ashley. "Can't you see she's lying? Tie her up and get the keys."

"She said she hid them," protested Heather.

"Check her pockets. See who's right."

Heather rose slowly and approached Lucy, who had no choice but to let her reach into her jacket pocket. If she moved a muscle, she didn't doubt that Ashley would shoot her.

"You were right," proclaimed Heather, pulling the keys out of Lucy's pocket and holding them up.

"And she didn't call the cops, either," said Ashley. "Tape her feet and hands," she ordered, adding a nasty chuckle. "When we're through, it will look like they had some kind of kinky sex game going on."

"No one who knows me will believe that," muttered Lucy, watching as Heather approached, ripping off a strip of duct tape. She grabbed the girl's arms just above the elbows and shoving her as hard as she could, propelling her across the room, toward Ashley. Ashley fired off a shot, and Heather screamed, dropping her gun and clutching her shoulder as she crashed to the floor. Lucy froze. Everything seemed to happen in slow motion as Ashley turned in her direction, preparing to shoot. She was raising the gun when Lenny sprang into action and charged across the room, taking her down with a crash that shook the entire ramshackle cabin.

Lucy immediately knelt beside Heather, who was screaming hysterically as blood spread across the white T-shirt she was wearing under the open raincoat. Fearing the wound was serious, Lucy quickly yanked the duct tape off Bart's hands and face. His legs were still taped to the chair, and to Sara, but by falling onto his knees, he was able to reach Heather to examine her wound. Lucy leapt across the room in two bounds and joined Lenny, who was struggling to hold Ashley down. She was fighting him with all the determination of a wild animal, biting and clawing, kicking and squealing, until Lucy finally succeeded in wrestling the gun out of her hand. "Be still right now or I'll shoot," threatened Lucy.

"Go ahead," screamed Ashley, still struggling to free herself. She was pinned beneath Lenny, who was lying on top of her, grasping both of her wrists. "Do you think I care? I want to die!"

"Shut up!" It was Bart. He was in his undershirt; he had stripped off his dress shirt and was using it to make a pressure bandage for Heather. "It's over. You're a disgrace. You're no daughter of mine. You deserve to spend the rest of your life in jail."

"What do you know?" Ashley screamed at him. "You don't know anything! Nothing's ever good enough for you! I hate you! I hate you!"

Sobbing, Ashley finally went limp, turning her face away and curling up into a ball.

Panting and still holding the gun, Lucy kept a wary eye on her as Lenny pulled his phone out of his pocket and finally called for help. When he finished, Lucy watched him pick up the second gun, which he held uncomfortably, waving it around the room. A sobbing Ashley no longer seemed to pose a threat, but Lucy didn't trust her and kept the other gun within reach as she began loosening the duct tape that still bound Sara and Bart. "Is she going to be okay?" she asked, with a nod to Heather.

"Yeah. It's a shoulder wound. Not life threatening," said Bart.

Heather's brimming eyes were fixed on her father. "I'm so sorry, Dad," she whispered, but Lenny didn't answer. He didn't even look at his daughter but stood silently, a man in deep shock.

Lucy tugged the last bit of tape connecting Bart and Sara, finally freeing them, and took her daughter in her arms. She hugged her close, stroking her hair, like she used to do when she was small.

Then, suddenly, there was a crash as Bart tackled Lenny, who fired off a wild shot as he fell to the floor. Lucy and Sara were shaking uncontrollably, watching as Bart gently unfolded Lenny's fingers and took the gun. Lenny didn't protest but lay still, exhausted, tears streaming down his cheeks.

"He was going to shoot himself," said Bart, by way of explanation, as he tucked the gun into his belt. "I was afraid he might do something like that."

"How . . . how'd you know?" asked Lucy. The shot was still ringing in her ears; she was stunned and struggling to make sense of it all.

"Because I feel like doing the same thing," said Bart in a matter-of-fact tone.

Lucy thought of the shame she'd felt at the police station the night Sara was arrested and figured that Bart and Lenny must be experiencing a similar emotion, magnified many times over. Shame and . . . what else? Loathing? Disgust? Horror? Betrayal?

Lucy hugged Sara tighter.

In the distance, they could hear the wail of sirens. Help was on the way.

Even the normally unflappable Detective Horowitz seemed troubled as Ashley and Heather were taken away. Heather went in an ambulance, handcuffed to the stretcher. Ashley, cuffed and shackled, was driven off in a cruiser, her composure restored as she calmly sat in the back, looking like Paris Hilton on her way to a costume party. Bart and Lenny were also gone: Lenny was on his way to a psychiatric clinic to be evaluated as a suicide risk, and Bart was completing his statement at the police station.

"I've seen a lot in my career, but this takes the cake," said Horowitz, seating himself beside Lucy on the cabin's porch steps. Sara was behind them, sitting with her back against the cabin wall and her legs stretched out in front of her.

Lucy was glad of his company. She felt small and fragile, as if she were made of glass, and found his presence protective and reassuring. "What will happen to them?" she asked.

"Oh, there'll be psychological exams and, no doubt, fancy lawyers, but in the end, they'll go to jail for a very long time, maybe life." He paused. "Ever since Columbine, the courts haven't had much patience with juvenile offenders, and since they're sixteen, they'll be charged as adults. And these are serious charges, the murder of Tina Nowak, kidnapping Sara and Dr. Hume, conspiracy to murder, conspiracy to kidnap, assault and battery. The list goes on and on."

"If the prosecutor can get a jury to believe two smart and attractive young girls actually did all these terrible things," said Lucy. "I was here, I saw them in action, and I can hardly believe it."

"I don't think the prosecutor will have any trouble convincing a jury at all," said Horowitz. "Ashley wrote it all down. We found a notebook in her backpack. It's all there. Lists of things to do, all checked off. Buy a blond wig, check. Get duct tape, check. Get sedatives from Dad's office, check. Drug Mom's coffee so she'll sleep. On and on, it's all here. It's damning."

How typical, thought Lucy, remembering how Sue had told her Ashley was obsessive about details. And just like a kid, too, to fail to consider the consequences of writing it all down and leaving a paper trail.

"Why did she do it? What was the objective?"

"To get out from under her parents," said Horowitz. "Simple as that. Ashley really hated the way they controlled her, and she managed to convince Heather to go along with her."

"It was all Ashley, really," said Sara. "She was the one who cornered me in the girls' room and made me go with them. Heather kept saying she didn't think it was a good idea. She even complained to Ashley that it wasn't fair that it was her mother who got killed and Ashley still had hers, even if she was in jail."

"Doesn't matter. Under the law, she's just as guilty as Ashley," explained Horowitz. He let out a long sigh. "But I agree that there are degrees of evil, and Ashley was clearly the instigator. She was relentless. She even planned to cut her father's nurse's brake line because the woman discovered the missing sedatives and questioned her about them."

Lucy gasped. "Amanda Connell died in a crash this morning."

Horowitz shook his head. "What a waste. Those girls had bright futures. If only they'd used all that energy for something positive. They might've found the cure for cancer. Who knows? Instead, they cooked up this crazy plan to eliminate their parents and anybody else who got in their way. Like it ever had a chance of succeeding."

"I don't know," said Lucy. "They came pretty close."

"Ashley thought of everything," said Sara.

"Not quite," said Lucy. "She forgot the school's new attendance policy. They call the parents whenever a student cuts class."

"Is that how you knew?" asked Sara.

"That attendance officer saved your life," said Lucy.

Sara was quiet, thinking. "Do you think I'll still have detention?" she asked.

"Absolutely," said Lucy.

CHAPTER TWENTY

On Sunday morning, Lucy was on her hands and knees, delving into the back of the closet to find her good black pumps, which she'd last worn at the Mother's Day brunch.

Bill found her like that, rump up. He stood for a moment, enjoying the view, before he spoke. "What on earth are you doing?"

Lucy's voice was muffled by the clothes hanging above her. "Looking for my good shoes."

"Why? It's Sunday."

Sundays at the Stone house were relaxing affairs, beginning with coffee and a leisurely perusal of the papers, followed by a big breakfast, which was worked off in the garden or on a long walk or bike ride.

"Exactly," said Lucy, emerging triumphantly with the shoes. "I'm going to church."

"What brought this on?" he asked. "You're not usually much of a churchgoer."

It was true. The family usually went to church only at Christmas and Easter.

"I don't exactly know," said Lucy, who was flipping through the hangers, trying to decide on something to wear. She was still a bit stiff and had a few bruises from her confrontation with Heather and Ashley at the cabin. "I guess I just want to hear that good is stronger than evil, something like that."

He stepped close and wrapped his arms around her waist. Lucy leaned back and relaxed against his broad chest, secure in his embrace. "Everything's okay," he said.

She turned and wrapped her arms around his neck, hugging him close. "I know, but it could have turned out a lot differently. Maybe I just need to say thank you," she said.

Out in the hallway, she bumped into Sara, sleepy-eyed and still in her pajamas. Her face and arms still bore red marks from the duct tape, and she was limping slightly due to sore, strained muscles.

"How come you're all dressed up?" she asked, squinting at her mother and scratching her head.

"I'm going to church," explained Lucy.

"Oh," said Sara, stepping into the bathroom. She turned and leaned against the doorjamb. "Can I come, too?"

"Sure," said Lucy, surprised. "But you'll have to hurry. I'm leaving in ten minutes."

Sara didn't make it in ten, so the church bell was ringing when Lucy found a parking spot on Main Street. As they hurried along the sidewalk, which tilted this way and that due to tree roots and frost heaves, Lucy began to have second thoughts. She and Sara had been in the news — they were part of a sensational story that had dominated the media for days — and she wondered how they'd be received. If she'd been alone, she probably would have turned right around and gone home, but she wanted to set a good example for Sara, so she marched on. Reaching the uneven granite steps that led from the sidewalk to the church, she instinctively reached for Sara's hand, just as she used to do when the kids were little and they needed help climbing up. When that happened, Sara usually snatched her hand away, but today she didn't do that. They were still holding hands as they approached the American Gothic arched door.

When they stepped inside, Lucy immediately saw that the church was crowded, but no heads turned, and the murmured conversations continued. The usher smiled warmly, welcoming them and giving them each an order of service. Only a few seats were left, and they slipped into a pew at the back and waited for the service to begin.

Soon the organist began playing the prelude, a variation on the old Shaker hymn "Simple Gifts." As Lucy listened to the familiar tune, the words came to her.

'Tis the gift to be simple,
'Tis the gift to be free,
'Tis the gift to come down where we ought
    to be . . .
To turn, turn will be our delight,
'Til by turning, turning we come round
    right.

That simple affirmation, combined with the moving organ music, was too much for Lucy, and tears sprang to her eyes. Embarrassed, she dug around in her purse for a tissue until Sara supplied one.

It had all come out right, she thought, gratefully. She and Sara both had some cuts and bruises and aches and pains from their ordeal in the cabin, but those were minor. It was the emotional scars that Lucy feared would be much slower to heal.

She simply couldn't understand why

things had gone so very wrong. Why had two talented and privileged girls behaved so wickedly, throwing their brilliant futures away like so much trash? What happened? Was it their parents' fault? Had Heather and Ashley simply erupted in reaction to their parents' relentless pressure to succeed? Or was society to blame, in all its crassness and materialism? Or had they been possessed by some demonic, evil force? She was hoping the church would provide some answers.

The procession was a welcome distraction from her thoughts, and Lucy sang along as the choir made its way down the aisle, singing "Faith of Our Fathers." It was a favorite she remembered well from her youth. Then came readings from the Old and New Testaments, a responsive reading, and recitations of the Apostles' Creed and the Lord's Prayer, both familiar and comforting to Lucy, who'd learned them as a child in Sunday school.

Then Rev. Sykes took the pulpit to deliver his sermon. He didn't begin immediately but stood, gazing out at the congregation and gripping both sides of the carved wooden lectern, which held the pages of his sermon.

"I see we're rather crowded," he finally said, prompting a ripple of laughter. "Per haps so many of you came because you are troubled by recent events in our town. I am troubled, too, and as I prepared my sermon this week, I thought I would talk about the problem of evil. But when I began to gather my thoughts on the subject, I realized I don't understand evil very well. Not many people do. In fact, when I did some research and looked the word *evil* up in the dictionary, I found a notation that the word is rarely used anymore. Evil apparently doesn't fit well with the modern consciousness.

"So I decided instead to talk about goodness, about love, but that subject also eluded me. I finally decided to speak about truth, because it seems to me that truth is the essence of God. Some say God is love, but unless there is truth, there cannot be love. And I would also venture to say that truth recognizes and banishes evil. And as we all know from the terrible tragedy that has rocked our town, evil does exist, even if we don't want to talk about it and call it by name. Evil thrives in the dark. It flourishes and grows in the hypocrisy and confusion created by lies. Evil withers when it is exposed to the bright, searing, healing light of truth.

"So I ask you to look into your hearts and root out the lies and half-truths you may find there. Now, more than ever, after all that has happened, we must be honest with ourselves and with each other. God's unconditional love is the greatest truth of all. I can't promise you nothing bad will happen to you, I can't promise that good will always triumph over evil, but I can tell you that no matter what, God loves you. And when we recognize that truth — that every being on this earth is valuable to God, is loved by God — we understand that we must also love one another, as God loves us. That is what we were put here to do. That is what God wants us to do, to simply love one another."

As she gathered up her things, Lucy pondered the minister's words. His sermon hadn't answered all her questions, but it had given her a place to start, she decided, resolving to put his words into action in her own life.

"Thank you for that sermon," she told the reverend when it was her turn to greet him at the door. "I was very troubled when I came here this morning, and you really helped."

"That's good to hear, Lucy," he said, grasping her hand in a hearty shake. "And it's good to see you when it's not even a holiday. I hope you'll come again."

"I will," said Lucy.

But Sara challenged her when they got back to the car. "Did you mean what you said?" she demanded. "Are you really going to start going to church?"

The question brought Lucy up short. "Probably not," she admitted, checking over her shoulder before pulling out and making a quick U-turn.

"You listened to a sermon about telling the truth, and you lied!"

"I think he knew I was fibbing. It was a social lie," said Lucy, driving along.

"Or maybe he believed you! Maybe he'll be standing at the pulpit next week, in an empty church, looking for you because you promised to come."

"I get your point," snapped Lucy, rather irked. But as she followed the familiar route toward home, she faced the unpleasant truth that she hadn't exactly been honest with Sara. She'd snooped in her room, checked her phone messages, and even searched her backpack. If Sara had kept a diary, Lucy admitted ruefully to herself, she would have read it.

"Okay," said Lucy, pulling up to a stop sign. "I have a confession to make. I've been worried about you, and I've done some things I shouldn't have, but I was afraid you were heading for trouble."

Sara looked surprised. "What exactly did you do?"

When Lucy had finished recounting her transgressions, Sara had just one simple question. "Why?"

"Elizabeth said you weren't sleeping, because of the phone. Zoe said you had laxatives. . . ."

"Mom, I tell you everything," protested Sara.

"Not true. What about the booze party?"

"I thought we were going to the movies. Honest. And about the rest, I told you about the photo and the rumors about me and Chad. . . ."

"What about the laxatives?"

Sara rolled her eyes. "They were for a report I had to do in health class on binging and purging."

Behind her, somebody honked.

"Oh," said Lucy, accelerating. "That's a load off my mind."

"You could have just asked me."

Lucy was chagrined. "From now on, I will," she promised, turning onto Red Top Road.

At work on Monday Lucy decided to follow Sara's advice. Instead of speculating and worrying about Ted's intentions, she came right out and asked him.

"Ted, are you planning to sell the paper?"

Across the room, Phyllis's severely plucked eyebrows shot up over her harlequin glasses.

"Why do you think that?" he asked.

"Well, I know a number of small weeklies have been bought up by big chains recently. And you've been gone a lot, and when you're here, you're very . . ."

"Picky," said Phyllis.

"That's the trouble with this business," he grumbled. "It's impossible to keep a secret."

"So you *are* selling the *Pennysaver*?" asked Lucy.

"No." He paused. "But I was."

"What happened?" quizzed Lucy

"Not enough money?" speculated Phyllis.

"Plenty of money."

"They weasled out of the deal," suggested Phyllis.

"Nope. I did."

"How come?" asked Lucy.

Ted looked around at the office, with its old-fashioned wood venetian blinds hanging in the plate-glass windows on either side of the door, the old Regulator clock on the wall, and the scarred vinyl tile floor, until his gaze finally settled on the rolltop desk he'd inherited from his grandfather, a legendary newsman.

"I guess what it came down to," he said, speaking thoughtfully, "is that I didn't want a corporation telling me what to do — what stories I could print, what ads I could or couldn't take. I want people in Tinker's Cove to know that the *Pennysaver* prints the truth, or as close to the truth as we can get."

Lucy and Phyllis were silent for a long minute.

"I was kinda hoping for health insurance," complained Phyllis.

"I think you made the right decision," said Lucy.

"Thanks," said Ted. "And since you're such an enthusiastic newshound, I know you're going to love your next assignment. It's a real investigative report involving fiscal mismanagement, wasted taxpayer dollars. It's a real stinking mess. Citizens are outraged and demanding action."

Lucy braced herself; this didn't sound good. "What exactly am I supposed to investigate?"

"The new sewage treatment plant. It's giving off foul odors, and the neighbors are furious."

"Yuck," said Lucy, grimacing.

■ ■ ■ ■

Everything was ready at the community center for the after-prom party. The Claws had set up their amps and mikes and were tuning up their guitars. The gym had been turned into a carnival, with games of all sorts. Video games were in one corner, trampolines in another; there was even a volleyball net. Refreshments had been set out: soft drinks, chips, and sandwiches were arranged on long tables, and pizzas were warming in the oven. There was even a make-your-own sundae bar, homemade cakes and cookies, and bowls of candy.

It was all ready, except for the chaperones. They were fading fast.

"This is past my bedtime," sighed Lucy. "Way past."

"I should never have let you talk me into this," said Sue, peering into a tiny purse-sized mirror, licking her finger, and smoothing her eyebrows. "I'm going to look absolutely awful tomorrow."

"Tell me again why I'm doing this," demanded Rachel. "I don't have a kid in high school."

"Yeah," said Pam, chiming in. "I finally got Tim out of the house. Why am I sitting

306

up all night, waiting for teenagers?"

"Because somebody had to take over where Tina and Bar left off, and because you're all wonderful, community-spirited people, solid citizens, and . . ." Lucy paused, letting out a big sigh. "I couldn't get anybody else."

"I understand Tina couldn't make it," said Sue. "After all, she can hardly rise from her grave, as much as she'd probably like to. But what's Bar's excuse? She's out of jail. She's a free woman, isn't she? And this party was her idea."

"She's been keeping a very low profile ever since Ashley's arrest," said Lucy, turning to Rachel. "What's going to happen to those girls? Is Bob defending Ashley?"

Rachel shook her head. "The Humes fired him when he suggested that Ashley accept a plea deal. They want to go to trial, and they think they can win since Heather is cooperating with the prosecution. They'll say it was all her idea, and now she's trying to put the blame on Ashley."

"But what about Ashley's notebook?" asked Lucy. "She had it all planned out, down to the last detail. She even had a list of things she planned to do once her parents were out of the way. She was going to move to New York, take a trip to Paris, and never,

ever play tennis again."

Rachel threw her hands up in the air. "You know Bar. She always gets her way. She won't give up. She's got a million rationalizations for Ashley's behavior."

"And Bart's going along with this, after what they did to him?" Sue was incredulous.

Rachel rolled her eyes. "He does what Bar tells him to do. She's been keeping him on a very short leash since he admitted his relationship with Amanda Connell."

"The one I feel sorry for is Lenny," said Lucy. "He gave that girl everything. I mean, he was driving that old wreck of a Volvo, and she had a brand-new Prius. He adored her."

"I don't know how you deal with something like that," said Pam, sadly. "Your own child turning against you."

"Oh, he seems to be coping okay," said Sue in a sardonic tone. "You'll never guess who I saw him with."

"Who?" asked Lucy.

"Elfrida!"

Lucy was still shaking her head over the vagaries of human behavior when the first kids started to arrive, still in their prom finery but toting duffel bags packed with comfortable clothes. One by one, they shuffled into the restrooms, where they transformed themselves from glamorous butterflies to average kids in T-shirts, jeans, and sneakers.

Lucy watched each new arrival, looking for Sara and one last glimpse of her beautiful dress. She was one of the last to arrive, accompanying Chad, who was resplendent in his tux and prom king crown. Sara, however, had no prom queen tiara. That was sitting on the platinum-blond head of Gerta Ingridsdottir, the Icelandic exchange student.

Lucy felt a pang of disappointment and hurried to console Sara. "You are so beautiful . . . I hope you're not upset."

"Upset? Why?"

"Well, because Chad's king and —"

"It's cool. Everybody loves Gerta, and she's going home next week."

"So you don't mind?"

"Not a bit."

"Did you have a good time?"

"It was terrific, except for Chad."

Lucy had expected this turn of events, but not quite so soon. "What about Chad?"

Sara leaned close, whispering into her mother's ear. "He's b-o-r-i-n-g. All he talks about is sports, especially baseball." Sara suddenly caught sight of Renee and waved to her, just as the Claws were beginning their trademark cover of "Sweet Caroline."

Sara was bouncing from one foot to the other. "Look, Mom, I wanna dance, okay?"

"Sure," said Lucy, watching as Sara joined a bunch of girls who were shimmying and shaking on the dance floor. The guys, she saw, were content to stand on the sidelines, watching and sipping sodas, before drifting off to the video games.

"Coffee?" Sue was holding two Styrofoam cups. "It's going to be a long night."

Lucy yawned, gratefully accepting the hot coffee. She took a sip, then chuckled.

"What's so funny?"

"I was just thinking about Toby and Molly. They can't wait for Patrick to sleep through the night so they can get a good night's sleep. But you know what? It never happens, does it?"

"Nope," agreed Sue, with a wry smile. "It never does. Even when they're all grown up, you're always waiting for that phone call in the night."

ABOUT THE AUTHOR

Leslie Meier is the acclaimed author of fourteen Lucy Stone mysteries and has also written for *Ellery Queen's Mystery Magazine.* She lives in Harwich, Massachusetts, where she is currently at work on the next Lucy Stone mystery.

We hope you have enjoyed this Large Print book. Other Thorndike, Wheeler, Kennebec, and Chivers Press Large Print books are available at your library or directly from the publishers.

For information about current and upcoming titles, please call or write, without obligation, to:

Publisher
Thorndike Press
295 Kennedy Memorial Drive
Waterville, ME 04901
Tel. (800) 223-1244

or visit our Web site at:

http://gale.cengage.com/thorndike

OR

Chivers Large Print
published by BBC Audiobooks Ltd
St James House, The Square
Lower Bristol Road
Bath BA2 3SB
England
Tel. +44(0) 800 136919
email: bbcaudiobooks@bbc.co.uk
www.bbcaudiobooks.co.uk

All our Large Print titles are designed for easy reading, and all our books are made to last.

HQ
MID-YORK LIBRARY SYSTEM
1600 Lincoln Ave.
Utica, NY 13502
(315) 735-8328

A cooperative library system serving Oneida, Madison
and Herkimer Counties through libraries

www.midyork.org

11